A Loving Presence

CATHLEEN ELLIS

Cover design by Launie Parry
Interior design by Veronica Yager

ISBN: 978-1629671239
Library of Congress Control Number: 2018937526

OTHER BOOKS BY CATHLEEN ELLIS

www.CathleenEllis.com

A Scarf of Promise

Castle in the Air

Making Our Way

Kara's Love

Baskets on Christmas Lane

Up To Me

Christmas Bright

A Voice for Gabby

Love Ties

Roses for Meredith

Old Crooked Road

Just Let It Go

Tend My Flowers

Together Now

Sky Tossed

A Humble Task

What's Beneath

Synopsis

In this sequel to *Roses for Meredith* joy, heartache, and reconciliation await Meredith and Colin.

Time does not diminish the caring they have for each other. Together they embrace a wonder-filled future.

1

December 1991

"We're bustin out proud of you, Meredith."

Meredith gazed at her dad, Uncle Milt, and Conner. They watched a big smile crinkle her face.

"Thanks, Uncle Milt."

The four of them joined together in a huggle, moving from side to side. They let go, giggling to each other.

"I'm so happy, you guys."

That December morning Meredith commissioned with other cadets. Families and friends stayed for a small reception of coffee, punch and cake in the same Student Union room where the commissioning took place.

"A second lieutenant in the United States Air Force," he paused, "that's got a nice ring to it," her dad mentioned with a nod to his head. Meredith heard the prideful sound of his voice.

That afternoon Meredith graduated from Kansas State University with a Bachelor of Science degree in Chemistry.

Two weeks before that she drove home to Porttown, Iowa, for Christmas with her family. The holiday arrived early for her because she had a report date of December 20. Colin stopped by for Christmas dinner after the family opened their presents.

"The men did it all this year," Meredith smiled to Colin.

"Oh yeah, I did the ham and scalloped potatoes," Conner added.

"I made the salad," Uncle Milt spoke up.

"Sorry guys, but I just couldn't do it, so I bought a chocolate satin pie and an apple pie," Jack said with a downturned look on his face.

Meredith touched his hand, "It's OK, Dad, we all understand."

She rolled her eyes and everyone broke into laughter; her dad never had baked a pie his whole life.

"I'm sorry I won't be there for your day, Meredith, your dad mentioned that your mom won't be coming."

"Right," she nodded to him, as she gave him her wide smile.

She saw a glint of sadness in Colin's eyes. She figured it came from having to miss two milestones of her life.

She touched his shoulder, "Got it, more important that you make it to that corn grower's meeting," she said as he watched her smile to him.

"Yeah, he's a state officer in that association; standing up for us and for our corn crops," she heard her dad say in the background.

The five of them ate dinner and demolished both pies. Meredith did dishes and put food away with Colin's help. They didn't cook so they helped with the cleanup. That was the way it played out at the Raymer house. Meredith got his coat and laid it on the chair. He needed to leave for another commitment. They stood next to the front door.

"I'll keep this Christmas meal in my memory, Meredith. It may be the last one we have together for some time. I'm so proud of you, your upcoming commissioning and graduation."

"I get that feeling too, Colin, an absence. I love you; I always will."

She looked up into his eyes, her tears starting.

He gathered her in his arms.

"You are a loving presence in my life, always with me, Meredith, and I love you," he whispered in her ear.

"What'll happen to us?" she choked out the words.

She watched him nod his head as he slowly released her.

"God knows, in His time, we'll know."

Meredith took her hand, pressed it to her heart three times and then touched Colin. Her hand felt the pounding of his heart.

ℴ

Beginning at Christmas 1992, Meredith and Colin exchanged holiday cards. Meredith got her card first.

"It's beautiful," she spoke out as she touched the sparkles on the card's snowy front, "this little red bird sitting on a branch of a leafless tree."

> Meredith,
>
> Golly, saw your dad and got your address. That's how we need to stay in touch, let your dad be our go-between. He said you'd send me your news. Harvest, great, still seeing Laura. I miss you and I love you. I'll be VP of our state corn grower's organization, installation's coming up soon. So there'll be meetings away from Iowa...as all corn growers unite, this stuff called ethanol, looks like one day it'll be a big deal for our crop.
>
> Love, Colin

Meredith's card arrived after Christmas.

"Oh Santa, you look so happy," Colin touched the front of his card, feeling positive about Meredith remembering him for the holiday.

> Colin,
> Sorry, this is gonna be late. Hope you had a good Christmas. I've been TDY, problem is I can't say much about what I'm doing, or where I'm at (lab rat stuff, high security). I'll save every Christmas card from you. Maybe some one day we can compare cards. You'll keep getting funny Santa Claus cards, keep sending me cards with a red bird on the front. It reminds me of Iowa in the holiday snow, with a cheerful bird in the skeleton trees. Tyler's been on my mind some lately, I guess because I'm in contact with pilots from time to time. Don't know if I ever fully thanked you for your kindness in visiting me at school after he died. You for sure were a part of my recovering from the sadness of losing him. Know you got a lot happening. I miss you and I love you.
>
> Meredith

Christmas 1994 arrived and they received their holiday cards.

Meredith,
Like the Santa, yeah, he's a cool dude, standing on the roof, ready to hop down the chimney...unbelievable, another year, another harvest, still seeing Laura. I really want to break away from Iowa and use my expertise elsewhere, a dream now, we'll see. I'm happy; hope you are as well. I love you and I miss you.

Colin

Hi Colin,
A beautiful bird card, I'm saving yours, year by year, in my memory chest. Asked dad not to share, so I could tell you. I've got my MS in Chemistry from Wright State University. The university's right next door; I'm at Wright-Patterson AFB, Ohio. I'm already helping to run laboratories, mostly national defense. Too busy right now to see anyone. I love my life. I miss you and I love you.

Meredith

The Holidays, 1996

Meredith,
Know this card will find you, your dad says you're traveling a lot. I have news (which I asked your dad to NOT share with you)...The Peace Crops wants me for two years, 1997-1999. I'm very excited; it'll be Africa, not sure where, but it's an agricultural assignment, crops, etc. Your family is taking over my farm operation 'til I get back. You know your dad, he tells me it's the right thing to do. Conner'll live at my place and keep it up. I love you and I miss you.

Colin

> Colin,
> Bird card is beautiful, WOW, what an experience you'll have! You're in my thoughts and prayers (as you've always been). I'll make Captain while you're away. And I'm enjoying the lab assignment (again, it's secure). I love you and I miss you.
>
> Meredith

The Holidays, 2000

> Dear Colin,
> Dad finally told me. We gotta go on, remember what we said about time (Christmas, 1991, before I headed out for my first assignment, it's in God's time, what happens to all of us). I know you were on top of the world after your Peace Corps assignment. I'm glad the Corps time went good. My family said you liked how they looked after your home and crops. They're the best, for sure. I love you and I miss you.
>
> Meredith

ℰℭ

> Dear Meredith, After what I've been through, I for sure understand that you are the only woman for me. What a frightful experience, I let my penis rule my head. Yeah, that's right, just getting back from the Peace Corps, and then thinking the woman was the right one for me....without even dating anyone else. Yeah, I know what you're thinkin' in your head, Colin don't beat yourself up, we all do things we later question/regret. Am I right? Yeah, I thought so. Your Santa, this year he's really got such a super smile, and a twinkle in his eyes. I love you and I miss you. Colin

The Holidays 2002

Dear Colin,
Unbelievable, losing Uncle Milt. I am so glad you were there
for him, dad told me. The docs always marveled at how well
Uncle Milt handled his disability (said the same thing about
Conner). Guess we've got tough genes, or something. I've
been at a lot of different bases, ramping up Air Force
effectiveness/safety, national defense, I'm getting a super high
level clearance, means I can't talk to you at all about what
happens. The country's a different place, unbelievable. Don't
know how it's affected you. I love you and I miss you.

> Meredith

&

Oh Meredith, the Santa card's so clever, don't know where
you find them. I waited for your card 'cause your dad says
you've been moved around so much, he wasn't even sure where
you were at the holidays...yeah I know you can't tell him much.
Corn's good; working at a national level now with the corn
grower's association. Also been working with Iowa State on
the latest and greatest corn seeds; both your dad and me have
fields connected with that research. I got plans, gonna do stuff
with the house; it's old. I love you and I miss you.

> Colin

&

"This is the third time I've been home in a month," she
told the taxi driver who dropped her at the family farm.

She and the driver were students in a couple of the
same classes at Porttown High.

"Christmas 2005's been unlike any year of my life."

"So sorry, Meredith, losing your dad and brother so
close together. Are you staying long?"

"Probably a couple of weeks, to get things settled."

"You got help?"

"Uh huh, my lawyer, my CPA (gosh, they worked with dad too), a wonderful neighbor, Colin Sanderson, and my dad's special friend, Jess."

Meredith opened the door to the only home she ever knew. She surveyed the insides, noting that her dad kept the wood floors looking good and the walls all painted.

"They did a great job," she spoke out as tears flooded her eyes, "with help from Jess."

Over the next few days she relied on Jess, who helped her have an estate sale. She donated everything else, except for three items which Jess took to keep for her, for someday.

"Do you think I've been too hasty about all the belongings, gosh about everything, Jess?"

"Time will tell Meredith, all I know is that you had to make sure details were handled the way you wanted them to; you're returning to your military life."

Before she left, Meredith made sure her ranch home got cleaned for renters who planned to move in February 1st.

"I'm just so numb right now," she said to Colin at her brother, Conner's, funeral. And the same words came when her dad died unexpectedly a few days later.

"Two funerals in two weeks, it's overwhelming for you," he held her close after her dad's memorial.

"Colin, you may not want to recall, but you had three funerals all close together, Cole's, then Ginny's and their baby's."

"Yeah, remember, I asked you to come to Cole's little gathering, right here in this same church reception area, all those years ago. Unbelievable we're going through this again."

₧

Meredith stayed at Jess's during this trip to Porttown. When the life insurance cleared from both her dad's and brother's deaths, she would have enough to pay off the taxes and mineral rights on the Raymer land for some time to come. Colin asked her if she wanted him to take over the corn operation for the family. She agreed, using her lawyer and CPA to get all the necessary paperwork ready. Meredith only saw Colin a couple of times while she was home, once for coffee in town.

"You grow more beautiful with time, dear one, and your eyes, a sheen I've not seen before," he shook his head to her.

Colin gazed again into her honey-colored eyes as they held hands at the shop.

"So handsome, so fit," she paused, swallowing hard, "so gracious to me through all this, oh Colin, thank you for everything. I appreciated that you wanted to deal with the lease on the house, but I decided a property management company needed to take care of that serious hassle. You got enough, doing our crop as well as your own."

"Thanks."

"I'm major now, and Colin, I've decided to stay for 20, so I have a decent retirement, gonna try to make lieutenant colonel."

She watched his smile to her, "That's so outstanding, Meredith, your dreams, they continue to unfold."

"And you've mentioned, you might want to run for the state legislature, more power to you, Colin. It'll be a load, but I know you can do it. Everybody knows you, from your work with the corngrowers, your commitment to 4-H, and to your community and county, the whole district, a deacon in church when you're here, wow."

"I wish I could stop time, Meredith. I don't want you to go."

"But I hafta, Colin," she nodded her head.

He noted her serious look, eyes unblinking and her mouth solemn.

"I love you, and I miss you, now more than ever, Meredith."

"I love you, Colin, you and me, we're a loving presence in each other's hearts."

He smiled to her, as the tears came into both their sets of eyes.

"You're with me always, in my mind, Meredith."

They got up and walked hand in hand out of the coffee shop.

"The property management place is down the street, gotta sign off on some paperwork, see ya, Colin."

They hugged and gave each other a gentle kiss.

"See ya."

They walked away from each other. Then they turned, smiled, and waved.

&

That evening Meredith and Jess fixed pizza and drank a good quantity of wine.

"Gotta get up early and head out but," she paused, "Jess, I want to thank you for the years you gave to dad, the two of you deciding not to marry, but to have a close and loving relationship, that included me, Uncle Milt, and Conner. I'm a little tipsy, but I'll tell you that I could one day see myself come back here. There's the farm, and the home, a lot to think about. And there's Tyler, the young man I loved back at college. His memory still surrounds me after all this time, first love; I'll love him for all eternity, in the still quiet place in my heart where all my loved ones will always be."

"I remember he came to be with you for Thanksgiving, a couple of months before his plane went down in a storm."

Jess turned to Meredith and their eyes connected, "Yeah, you really cared about him. Your dad saw your love, and so did I."

Jess touched her arm as they sat next to each other on the couch. They watched the fire with its dying red embers, still warming their toes.

"It's been good for us to have this conversation. I'm gonna talk to grief folks here, to help me through all this sadness, anger too. I would hope you'll get counseling wherever you are, Meredith. You've suffered a terrible loss," she paused, "no, two losses, the only Raymer left. You looked at the card your mom sent to me for you?"

"I did, she wrote a heartfelt note. I'm happy for her, going on with her life, she's been very successful with her florist business. She'll have a lot of sadness for awhile." She paused and nodded to Jess, "I'll get help, the military takes care of its own, so much sadness since 9-11-2001."

The Holidays 2008

Dear Colin,
Need to get this to you with my current address. So life keeps twisting and turning. It's over with the guy. I'm kinda like you, you're the only person for me in my life. I'm teaching chemistry at the Air Force Academy in Colorado Springs, plus getting my teaching credentials at the University of Colorado, Colorado Springs. What I've got left is student teaching. One day I THINK I will want to work with high school students, that's when I retire from the military. Now that looks three years out. I really enjoy working with the Academy cadets; they're driven, and still so enmeshed in the whole conflict in the Middle East. Some will see duty over there as soon as they graduate. My red bird card, so neat. I love you and I miss you.

Meredith

ஐ

Dear Meredith,
Got your card and the jolly Santa, gosh, I'm just so sorry things didn't work out for you. Jess told me. I bet you decide on some high powered assignment, in some lab where your chemistry expertise can make a difference. I think I like being a state representative for Iowa from our district. The politics are crazy; it ought to be an interesting ride, just like your Air Force career's been. Hey, my constituents're already encouraging me to make a run for US House of Representatives, for Iowa. Unbelievable, because I just got

> elected to the state house! You're always with me, in my heart
> and mind, time isn't diminishing that. I love you and I miss you.
>
> Colin

Late November 2011

She settled into her apartment, in a new complex in Porttown. Meredith decided on a six-month lease and had the little bit of furniture and possessions she owned shipped from her final Air Force assignment. She wanted to stay in one place, after 20 years of moving from base to base and laboratory to laboratory.

"My retirement ceremony, I kept it brief, for my lab rat associates, and me.

I was definitely ready to move on, to do work where I could talk to people about what I do, not all the secrecy that was always there in my assignments."

Meredith and Jess sat across from each other at an early evening retirement dinner she wanted to do for Meredith. Meredith picked the restaurant.

"I'm your family, now, Meredith. I'm adding up the years, you'll be 39, in a month?"

"That's right, I have a whole new life to live."

"Any place you'd rather be?"

Jess watched her shake her head.

"Nah, I used to tell folks, after about year 12 in the Air Force, that I've served in some great and unusual locations, but end of the day, here, my roots, Iowa corn, snow, the land," she paused and smiled, "this is the place where I'm meant to be."

"Talked to Colin yet?"

'Nope, he's due back before long, not sure when his round of corn grower meetings will recess for the holidays. You're giving me that look. I know communication is instantaneous with a cell phone, but honestly, I hate the phone, too many calls and too many life disruptions with the military."

"So you'll wait to hear from him?"

"Uh huh, when the time is right."

"It's still early; I want to show you a couple of things before I return you home."

Jess drove the two miles from town to the Raymer home. Meredith stood in front of the empty lot, a sadness gagging her throat. The burning lump rose up into her nose, making her cough and cry at the same time.

"Oh Jess, I never knew exactly what happened after the fire."

"Colin took care of everything."

"He shared a little, got our family lawyer and CPA involved, 'cause there was fire insurance."

"Yeah, it was a complete tear down and take away. He seeded the whole area with native grass."

"Looks like a house never even stood here; man, like the fire took our trees too," Meredith shook her head to Jess.

"Uh huh, I think that was his intent; he didn't want you seeing any of the damage to the home or landscape. Now there's just the barn in the distance."

Jess breathed out and spoke in a stuttering voice, "That was after Jack and Conner left us. Oh my gosh you just had so much on your plate."

"Jess, would you give me a minute?"

She touched Meredith's arm, "As much time as you need."

Meredith noticed the dried ground after the last snow. She walked around the area, trying to remember her home. A mash of memories started hitting her, scrolling through her mind, spinning her back through time.

"I had a good life here, God," she whispered, "but I was gone at 16, so young, immature, but I held on. Now here I am, back. Thank you for my life."

She knelt, the cold hard ground cutting into her knees. She prayed, sensing a sharp wind whipping against her face. Meredith roused, got up, and moved toward the car.

"Jess, pretty rough, the memories, so many and vivid. I'm glad you brought me here. I needed to see this."

They drove back down the county road toward town. "And Colin's."

They both got out and walked up the stone path toward the front porch.

"Oh, wow, oh my gosh, what happened, Jess? I don't recognize anything about the Sanderson place. I helped fix up the roses at the front and sides of the house after Cole died. I see now, uh, it looks like there are trimmed rose bushes to the side. I tried to help Colin get his feet on the ground after so much sadness."

"A few years back Colin had a completely new home built, over the foundation, which he widened and lengthened. He planted trees, has a summer rose garden, besides what you just saw. He's done a lovely job on the inside of his home. Colin sought my help one summer after I'd finished teaching a summer session at school. Jack liked what we did."

"Colin never mentioned," she shook her head as she looked at Jess.

"I know, Meredith, there was only so much you could say in your holiday cards."

"He told you about the cards we exchanged?"

"Oh yes, he's become," she paused and smiled, "like a son to me, as you've come to rely on me. Jack made Colin feel like a member of the Raymer family."

"Jess, times like this, I miss dad, Conner, Uncle Milt."

Meredith and Jess hugged as Meredith's burning tears of memories fill her eyes.

"It's cold, time I was getting back to my place. Thank you for the lovely dinner, Jess, and showing me the outside of Colin's home."

Jess left her off in front of her apartment, "One day at a time, OK Meredith, otherwise, your new life, it'll be overwhelming. Maybe we can get together over the Christmas vacation. You'll have news to share."

Meredith nodded and waved to her friend before Jess drove off.

§∅

She glanced at her cell phone for the time.

"Wow, this is a brand new building, not old Porttown High. I better hustle." She strode through the wide front doors to the school and stopped by the front office to get her visitor's pass.

"Welcome, Miss Raymer, to Porttown High."

She exchanged greetings with the principal and the chairperson for all the sciences at the high school. They showed her the chemistry classroom and shiny laboratory area. And Meredith answered their questions. She sensed that both men were kid people and interested in their students and their mental as well as physical well being. Meredith concluded the interview by asking for the part-time position in chemistry, one regular class and one AP chem, for the spring semester. She expressed interest in the morning classes; it would give her a half day to work on her farm and planting her corn crop.

"It will be a challenge, one which I would enjoy," she nodded as she shared with both men.

She thanked them for the opportunity to interview.

"We'll be making our decision in a few days, and we'll contact you, whether you get the job or not. You were smart to get your Iowa secondary science education certificate."

"First time in twenty years I applied for a job out in the civilian world, we'll see," she nodded as she made her way out of the high school.

She walked to her car in the school parking lot whispering, "I have a new life in a place where I want to be; I must cherish every moment of it."

§∅

"Meredith, hello, welcome."

"Oh my gosh, Colin, you're back, it's so good to hear your voice."

"Yours too, want to invite you to dinner at my place tomorrow evening. Bring your holiday cards; I've saved all of mine. We have to celebrate, your retirement and return to us."

"Yeah, I'm free, dress up?"

"Uh huh, used to wearing a coat and tie, after three years in the legislature."

"And I'm used to a uniform; this'll give me a chance to wear an outfit I've saved for a special occasion. What can I bring?"

"I'm grilling steak, so a red wine, sound good?"

"Great, I'll check my supply and bring one. I tried to buy wine of some kind at every out-of-country place I worked at."

ℛ

Meredith drove her SUV to Colin's about 10 minutes early for their dinner together. She wanted to take a look around his place in the daylight.

"Wow, he added a second story, and a porch that wraps around the entire house. He wanted an older-time look, even though the house must just be a few years old," she thought as she drove slow down the lane from the highway.

She parked outside in front of the three car garage.

"Oh, I saw them the other night, but they didn't register in my brain. But now, I see, yeah, the rose bushes, oh my gosh, his mom's roses. He must have done these, to remember her by."

She walked up the path to the front door.

"Our roses," tears misted her eyes, "they got burned up in the fire," she remembered only grass where her home once stood.

She rang the door bell. Soon Colin opened the door, and they stood in front of each other. Time paused; they looked into each other's eyes, with memories flying about like swirling snowflakes.

"Oh, come in; it's just so awesome to see you, Meredith."

All she could do was nod and blink back tears.

He closed the door and they came into each other's arms.

"Colin, these are happy tears, it's hard to fathom this."

"I know; I could only imagine this day coming," he paused, "and it has."

They separated and he took her coat, hanging it in the closet near the front door.

He took her hands in his, "Almost 20 years, Meredith, Christmas, 1991. You're more beautiful now than you were at 19, your honey eyes and shining hair, I'm glad you've kept it longer and curled, and your green dress, nice."

"Your hair's darkened, but you keep it short, it's still blonde. Those blue eyes, same eyes, time's been really really good to you, hard work's only helped make you more handsome, you in your blue blazer and gray slacks."

"May I show you around?"

2

Late November 2011

"Certainly."

Colin took her, room by room, through his home. She noted the beautiful wood flooring throughout.

"I don't use some of the rooms, so it's pretty easy to keep everything up."

"It's a lovely country home; tell me how this all happened, 'cause you didn't say much to me."

They stood in the kitchen with its stainless steel sink and appliances and the big island in the middle. Colin laid out an appetizer of small slices of apples and slices of sharp cheddar cheese. He opened the wine, this one from Meredith while she worked in Italy. They cheered each other and drank from the wine glasses.

Colin shared the story of his home's deconstruction. He salvaged some of the flooring, capturing the old wood and using it on several floors in the new home as he had it constructed. He also mentioned that his new home was completely paid off.

"The old place, bad wiring, old plumbing, it had to all go. I'm so happy with this, just not much furniture. Jess helped me with the interior design. Do you like what she decided for me?"

"Very much, simple, modern, everything with clean lines. I especially like that you have a large guest bedroom and bathroom on the main floor, plus your study. The fireplace is marvelous, my favorite part of the great room."

"You know why I have a bedroom on the first floor?"

"Yeah," she looked him in the eye, smiling, "years and years away, you'll not want to be climbing that set of 11 stairs to the second floor."

He nodded to her, "Fer sure, my folks could'a never climbed them as they got sicker."

They stood out on the back porch as Meredith watched Colin barbecue the thick filet mignons. They wore heavy jackets Colin pulled from the mud room area near the back door.

"Salad?"

"In the frig, second shelf, and the rolls are on top of the microwave."

Meredith admired the beautiful table setting, the snow white tablecloth and the tapered red candles.

She choked up, and with a wavering voice asked, "These your mom's dishes and silverware?"

"Uh huh, I've kept a set of 8 of everything and use them only occasionally."

She touched his arm as they prepared to sit down near each other. Meredith poured more wine as Colin popped a bottle of champagne.

"To Meredith, whose loving presence was always with me."

She moved her glass to his, "To Colin, whose loving presence will forever be with me."

They sipped champagne and proceeded to devour steak, potatoes, salad and rolls.

"I'm starved; this all tastes so wonderful. I haven't cooked hardly at all these past years, this home-cooked meal, marvelous," she nodded to him.

She could hear soft music in the background, "What a wonderful sound, who is it?"

"Enya, I love her stuff."

They talked, mainly Colin explaining to her some of the work he did the past three years in the state legislature.

"You have," she paused and looks at him, "how much time left in your term?"

"A year, 2012, a year of redistricting, don't think it'll affect my district much. But I have a dream that I'd like to share with you some time."

"Not now?"

"Nope, not the right time."

They finished dinner.

"Same old rule applies; you cooked, so I clean up."

"Good, I'll get the fire started; we'll get cozy on the couch, bring along the champagne, wine and your holiday cards.

"Dessert later?"

"Uh huh."

Meredith put dishes in the dishwasher, washed and dried a couple of pans, and set new forks and spoons at the table for dessert. She refolded the napkins for later use and blew out the candles Colin lit for the meal.

"Gas fireplace is great, Colin, but you can still use wood, right?"

"Yeah it's a combo. Grab your glasses. I see you put your cards next to mine."

Meredith sat near him as they looked into the blaze of logs. He turned and pulled something from the floor.

Meredith held the red rose bud, starting to cry. She smelled the spicy scent and put her hand to her face. Her memory spun her back to sitting on her bed in the dorm, holding first one rose bud and then another, from two different young men. She paused and put the rose bud on the arm of the couch, but kept her hand on it.

"Uh uh," she paused, "do you remember, that memory just hit me, standing in the dorm reception area, as you walked up to me and handed me a red rose bud?"

She turned to him as he nodded, "Indelibly etched in my brain, forever."

"Oh Colin, thank you, for that day, that weekend, you helped me so much after Tyler's death. We went to church together the next morning, and then, well, then we both just got on with our lives."

"Yes, we did."

They held each other close, Colin's lips descending on hers. They kissed, a long tongue-teasing kiss, exploring each other's mouths, again and again. They both caught their breaths as they moved their lips away from each other. They calmed and looked into each others eyes.

"Meredith, I've wanted to ask you this for so many years."

"Ask?"

He watched her eyes widen.

"Meredith Raymer, will you marry me?"

"Yes, Colin Sanderson, I most certainly will marry you."

"This home, I want it to be a place of love, of happiness. I built it, always thinking of you one day being here with me."

"And I will be."

"Let's leave this wine and champagne. Oh Meredith, I want you, I've always wanted you, in my dreams, in my waking hours."

"As you've been in the back of my sexual mind, all these years."

They darkened the living room and dining area and left a light on in the kitchen. Hand in hand they ascended the stairs to Colin's bedroom. Meredith felt a sharp burning in her groin that moved up and up into her throat. They took their time, undressing each other as Meredith heard the quiet background music.

"I've waited for this time a lot of my life, Colin."

"I know," he smiled down to her as they stroked each other's backs and buttocks. He moved his erect penis, pressed it to her stomach and held her breasts in his hands. He picked her up and laid her gently on the bed, on the special sheets he saved for this time. They kissed and caressed, moving their hands over each other's bodies.

Meredith nodded her head as she felt her groin continue to flame. She smiled up into his passion-filled eyes.

She felt his warmth, stretching her and stretching her, as he slowly filled her. They began thrusting together, in slow motion, then faster and faster until they spoke each other's names and exploded together in their orgasms.

"I love you, Meredith," she heard his husky voice.

"I love you, Colin," she whispered back to him. "I, I was so scared, twenty years passed; we've changed so much, didn't know for sure how we'd react to each other after all that time."

Side by side they held each other close as they kissed and felt the moldings of each other's bodies.

"I want you with me, every morning and every night, now, and when lines fill our faces and silver rules our hair."

She kissed him and whispered, "That's the way our grandkids will see us."

"Uh huh, we're gonna be older grandparents, I'm 45 now and you're almost 39."

Their hunger for each other grew with each touch. Meredith climbed on Colin and proceeded to kiss his face and neck. They came together again, crying out each other's names as they climaxed. Sleep took them for a little while. And then they nestled in each other's arms again.

"Hungry?"

She kissed his neck and nodded, "It's time for dessert, and card reading, and more time in front of the fire."

Meredith rolled up the sleeves of Colin's sweatshirt that hung down to her knees. He found an old pair of sweatpants to go along with the shirt. He wore his old Iowa State sweat gear. They descended the steps, Colin with his arm around her shoulder and Meredith holding tight to his waist.

"You remembered socks," Meredith smiled up to him as she sat on the couch.

"Course, I don't want you to catch cold, young lady," he said in a fatherly-sounding voice.

They finished off the champagne and drank the last of the bottle of wine from dinner as they went through their holiday cards together.

"How in heck were you able to hang on to the cards?"

"Colin, I kept a little memory chest, for special cards, yours, from dad, Conner, mom."

"Oh my gosh, I don't even remember sending this card to you at all, Meredith, read the inside, please."

She read the paragraph, "Yeah, this musta been one super hard card to write," she shook her head to Colin. "None of my business, but is this former wife in the area?"

"Nope, moved on to other adventures."

"Yeah, that's what happened to the officer I had the mighty short marriage with."

They continued reading the cards and pulling up memories from the past 20 years.

"Stay with me, Meredith, the rest of the night, I'll switch the log off and close the damper."

"OK, Colin, I'm suddenly just absolutely beat. Can we save the dessert, have it for breakfast?"

"Awesome idea, see you upstairs, I'll turn off the lights down here."

They snuggled in bed together, their hands on each other's bodies.

"I have lots of touching to do, to memorize your beautiful body, Meredith."

"Me too, for you, you're tall, strong, and so fit."

"Aim to stay that way too, sweet one, it's after 1:30."

They spooned together as they drifted into sleep. Hours later Meredith shot upright in bed, wide awake. She turned and saw Colin beginning to wake up. As she always had, the first thing in her morning, she went to the window to discover the morning light gleaming on the branches of the skeleton trees in Colin's back yard.

"What a beautiful setting," she whispered as she watched the sun peeking above the horizon, "purple, pink, blue, orange, magenta, all those colors at this sunrise, wow."

"I heard your description, Meredith, come back to bed and keep me warm. Are our skies most wonderful?"

"Oh my gosh, they are. I don't remember the skies from my youth."

She crawled back into bed after she pulled off the big sweatshirt.

"That's because we were too busy trying to figure out our lives. You were pretty much gone at 16, don't think you even took the time to look up at the skies."

"Absolutely correct."

They held each other tight, kissing and kissing. In their delight they became one again. While Meredith showered, Colin started the coffee.

"Wow, you're quick, sweet one."

"Uh huh," she pecked his cheek, "it's a military thing, getting ready to head out somewhere at the drop of a hat, so no, I don't waste water."

She stood next to him, in her beautiful green dress, her hair back behind her ears. He noticed the tiny star earrings, and kissed each of her ear lobes.

"I'm starved."

"Yeah, knew you would be," he paused, "and guess what, dessert is first. I couldn't remember what you liked besides pie and cake, so I baked a cherry pie, not mine, but frozen from the store, best I could do."

They stood together, drinking coffee and waiting for the cherry pie to heat up in the microwave.

"So, what else are we having besides pie?"

"Eggs and toast, bacon if you want."

They sat next to each other at the dining room table, as Meredith had left it the night before. With their warm cherry pie, they had vanilla ice cream.

"Yeah, dessert first, Colin, I love it."

They brought their next course, bacon, eggs and toast and finished that off with coffee.

"You like coffee, Meredith."

"I do indeed, this is my third cup; back in the day, in my old world, well, all of us lab rats drank coffee by the many gallons. It kept us sharp, uh, the caffeine did. I don't know anybody in any of my groups who used uppers or downers to help them along. We were drug-tested, all through my years in the military. All the deployments, the quick entries and exits into all the work we had to do, no matter where we were, had to be always alert."

She paused, shaking her head.

"Sorry, didn't mean to give you such an extensive explanation."

"Understood," he touched her hand, then brought it to his mouth and kissed the back of it, "in a while you'll get back into the civilian world."

"You need to know this about me, Colin, I'll always be military, always will love what I did, oh, the memories. I'll need to watch that I'm not ordering someone around. That'll piss off folks out here in my new world."

Colin chuckled at her comment.

"You're so blunt, straightforward, but I love that about you, Meredith."

"That's right, too direct, I'll be happy to work with young people, be able to temper my mouth, yea my big mouth, with the younger ones. I'm just so used to giving orders to other adults."

"What goes on for you today?"

"Fixin' my place up for the holidays. For many years I did not even have a Christmas tree because I was TDY and living in a temporary base housing situation. So this year, I want to do a proper tree with decorations, and buy presents, for you and Jess. Lots of years I didn't even get presents for my family. I sent dad a check and told him to get what Uncle Milt and Conner needed, and of course, something for him."

Meredith caught her breath, as the tears coursed down her cheeks. She put her head down and sobbed. Colin took her hand and held it.

She raised her head, "This still happens to me, Colin, a smack of sadness, of missing my family, of missing Tyler, it just hits me. I have to stop what I'm doing and work through the pain. I mean, after all this time, it will get better, right?"

He grabbed tissues from the kitchen counter.

"Thanks."

As she blew her nose and coughed up the congestion in her throat, he nodded to her.

"Time, like we talk about, it takes time."

"And you, Colin, what's your day going to be like?"

"OK, I know you don't know anything about my legislative activity."

"That's right."

"So here's how my yearly calendar's been working out, like for the past three years," he paused, "I spend a lot of time January into early May in Des Moines."

Meredith nodded her head, "My guy, a member of the Iowa House of Representatives, wow."

They laughed together, Colin seeing Meredith's googily eyes.

"Yeah, sometimes it's hard for me to believe too."

"So tell me."

"I share a two bedroom apartment just a few blocks from the capitol, with a fellow legislator, he's single and pays half while he's in town. I just keep signing a year's lease, 'cause sometimes I'm in Des Moines for other business the rest of the year, when the legislature isn't in session. It's good to have a place. It's within walking distance of just about everywhere I need to be. And I have a small office at the state capitol."

"Corn planting?"

"Hey, that's tricky as hell, 'cause we're near the end of the session, and we for cripes sakes are always running behind, like this year we got way behind and the legislative session extended into May a bit. It was crazy; the corn got planted kinda late. I've got a great part-time employee, a retired guy who happens to like helping out during busy times, like planting and harvesting."

"You not only had your corn to plant, but you had all our Raymer land to plant."

"That's right, but we handled it. You just do what you gotta do. I survived."

He smiled to Meredith and took her hand, "Does it look to you like I've suffered from any of that?"

She giggled to him, "Nah, not at all."

"It's almost December, so we've got the fields as set as we can for April planting. We gotta let the moisture take hold; the snow's so super important. Now that you're home for good," he stopped and hugged her shoulder as they sat at the table, "please talk to your CPA and lawyer, to shift all the farming stuff over to you. I just stood in until you retired; it's important, OK?"

She saw his serious look and heard his determined voice.

"Yeah, it's on my list of things I must do."

"So, you understand how this will play out, Meredith, I've been pretty much gone part of the year. To answer your question about what I'm doing right now, well it's the prep for being gone. Except now, with you here, and our wedding coming up, I'll come home more, quick weekends, with my dear one."

"You haven't shared, are you going to try for a third term in the state legislature?"

"Uh huh, I want to try, and after that," he stopped.

He watched Meredith nod to him. She looked deep into the pools of his blue eyes, as if reading his mind. He saw her mouth became straight and firm.

"I can see, as plain as day, you'll get reelected, 2012, for a third term, and then, after that, you'll step up to the US House of Representatives from the state of Iowa. I can help you do that, Colin, and I want to."

They stood and came together in a hug.

He bent his head and kissed her, "You with me, every day, every step of the way."

They returned to their hug.

She looked up into his face as they separated, "I'm so excited, and happy for you, Colin."

"That halo of love, Meredith, it still surrounds you, as it always has."

℘

Meredith and Colin made a plan to stay together several nights a week during December. Meredith put up her Christmas tree the first day of the month, wanting to leave it up into 2012. She looked at the bare tree, and a memory caught her.

"I wonder if dad and Conner put the Christmas decorations back in the barn, these past years, like I did the last year I was home. I remember telling them where I would keep the ornaments."

That prompted Meredith to get into grubbies and revisit the Raymer property. The morning held cold and crisp as she watched the clear blue sky on the way to her old place. Colin gave her a key to the side barn door. He kept a key as well as did the hired man who helped him.

Meredith left the door open to let the outside light guide her back to the office area and the apartment where Uncle Milt lived.

"Sure don't remember where the inside barn lights are," she spoke out. She found the office and looked around, opening up the empty desk drawers and filing cabinet.

"Dad, it's empty, but your office looks as neat, orderly as you always left it, so's the barn area. Colin and Jess must'a taken the few things from the barn, but he's kept the electricity on."

She stepped out and went over to the apartment door.

"Nothin's left of Uncle Milt's stuff, just a bare couple of rooms, gotta get out of here, the memories, me doing my chemistry experiments, and dad nearby doing his bookwork."

She finally found the light switch for the overhead barn lights and turned them on. After getting herself oriented, she looked at a set of shelving in one corner.

"Oh my gosh, Dad, thank you for putting the Christmas ornaments away out here," she said as she pulled the dusty box marked Christmas from a shelf that was near her height.

Before she opened the box, her tears began again.

"God, you kept these safe, for a time when you must'a known I might try to find them again. These precious ornaments, one of the few things left from my past, thank you, Lord," she whispered.

She walked with the box back to the nearly empty office. She grabbed a tissue from her pocket to wipe away her tears.

"Time to take a peek."

With care Meredith removed each ornament and set it on the desk. After five minutes, she saw them all, each one with a special memory for her.

"Keep these safe," she spoke out as she repacked them, "this is part of my Raymer world. I sold or gave away everything else, kinda in haste, after Conner and dad died." She paused and let out a big breath, "I sure wasn't thinkin' straight right then, so glad these were put away. I flat forgot about them."

On her drive back to her apartment with her newfound treasure, the memory of her brother's and dad's deaths hit her again.

"Hey, I've done nothing; I'll get out to their graves, not been there yet, oh my gosh since their funerals. I need to order Christmas wreaths from the Flower Shop. I must honor my family, Uncle Milt too. I'm not really alone, no I'm not. My family, while I was in the barn, I could almost hear them speaking to me, from here, in my heart."

Meredith found a radio station that played Christmas music. Between bites of her pb&j and drinks of coffee she strung the multicolored lights and hung the family ornaments on the tree. She sang along with the radio songs.

The call she answered was short and to the point. Afterward she set her cell down and danced around her apartment, twirling in a waltz, her arms raised, with Colin as her imaginary partner.

"Delight, the delight in my life, it continues to exceed my expectations," she shouted.

ℰↃ

Colin watched her all through dinner that night.

"This lasagna is so excellent," he paused, "And the wine, smooth and fruity, just perfect with the food and the garlic bread."

"Glad you like the main dish, Colin, 'cause it's from the grocery store freezer. I just can't compete with a couple of brands that just do an excellent job, especially with Italian food."

"You're so excited, Meredith, it's a glow in your eyes, same one I saw when I asked you to marry me."

"I am, meet with the teacher I'm replacing tomorrow afternoon. I'll get my class rosters and his lesson plans for spring semester plus the textbooks. I gotta get going on how to handle the rest of the year, especially how to share the chemistry laboratory with the other chemistry class, and how to prep my AP chem kids for their AP exam."

"What's the deal, with the two classes, the teacher?"

"Yeah, teacher's wife's been transferred to another ConAgra facility in the Midwest. He's headed out with her; no kids, so it's simpler. He helped coach, so reason he just had two classes. Another teacher at Porttown High teaches the third chemistry class, plus handles all the physics."

"Do you have a contract?"

"Uh huh, they've decided I'm 52%, (figuring in a planning period which I hope I won't always need), so I've got health insurance, as a supplemental." She paused, "I'll use my VA medical."

"That's good, I've just got my own health insurance policy; it's expensive," he nodded to her.

"Coffee with your dessert?"

"Decaf?"

"Yeah, it is, neither one of us want to be awake all night."

They cleared the small table and cleaned up the dishes from the meal.

"Oh, cheesecake, I love it, but I never think to have it."

"I'm glad you like it, because I stand in the grocery store and try to figure out what I need to cook and bake, not having done any of this since I lived at home." She paused and smiled to him, "What I remember, Colin, is how proud you were when you learned to cook different kinds of meat, that's after Cole died."

"Yeah, he did all the cookin' at our home after the folks were gone, so I cooked from remembering him and mom working in the kitchen."

Meredith heard the wavering of his voice.

"We never really get over the permanent absences of our families," she nodded.

They took their coffee and dessert and sat on the loveseat in Meredith's living room.

"The tree, colorful, so bright, new ornaments?"

"Nope, sent up some dust clouds as I found my family's ornaments in a box on some shelving in the barn. It's where I asked dad to keep them the last Christmas I was home. I never dreamed they'd still be out there. He and Conner must've remembered my request, from 1989 forward."

She turned to Colin, "It still gets me, the ornaments, one of the last remnants of my early days."

He watched her put down her dessert next to her coffee. She wiped the tears streaming from her eyes.

"For some reason the ornaments, well, they invoke so many memories, swirlin' in my head."

He put his arm around her and held her close. He watched her touch the rose he gave her the night he asked for her hand in marriage.

"Gonna dry it?"

"That's right, it's a rose with such memories, our first night, as we began our life together."

Much later Meredith helped him on with his coat.

"Sorry I can't stay the night; I gotta be up and out early for a retreat with the men in our church."

"I understand, I love you, Colin. We just barely got through our dessert and coffee."

He lifted her chin to his lips and kissed her.

"Our passion, it fills us up, keeps us wanting each other again and again. I love you, dear one."

They hugged. She watched him turn and wave to her as he walked toward his car. She waved back.

⅋

The church service that Sunday took her back to her last weeks before the university, all those years ago. She played her French horn with the choir. That sound was absent with this church choir. As she walked out, she looked about at the congregation. Very few faces looked familiar to her.

"The choir sounded wonderful, and I enjoyed your sermon," she spoke after she introduced herself to the minister.

"Welcome back, Meredith; it's certainly a different world, and church, from what you knew."

"That's right, I'm anxious to get involved with the church of my youth. I'll be attending, as much as I can, will be in touch with you."

Meredith's spirits lifted as the snowy Christmas holiday approached.

"Hey, I once worked in this flower shop, a lot of years ago. I remember making up wreaths. It'll feel so good to be able to go see my families' graves," she spoke to the helper at the Flower Shop. She gathered together the three wreaths she ordered several days earlier.

The helper replied, "The wreaths look super at the graves with the snow on the ground. It feels like we're celebrating Christmas with our loved ones."

The young lady saw Meredith raise her eyebrows and give her a wide smile.

Meredith nodded, "Hey, you're right, I will be celebrating Christmas with my loved ones."

She stopped by Porttown High before she drove to Landview, the Porttown cemetery.

"Jim Parter," he held out his hand to Meredith as they met in the Chemistry Lab.

"Meredith Raymer," she nodded as she shook his hand. "Oh, this little chem lab looks really nice; you've kept it up."

"I share the lab with the teacher who has all the Physics classes here and the third chemistry class. So we do our best to clean up after each other. He's a real neat nick; I'm not so much," he smiled to her as they found two stools.

"I think this is most everything you'll need: my gradebooks, uh everything's also on the computer which I'll show you in a minute, the textbooks which are critical; it's all set up in PowerPoint, from the publisher. You may want to embellish things a bit?"

She smiled, nodding her head, "I expect so."

"What's your background, Meredith?"

"Retired military, lieutenant colonel, after 20 years, I'm into the next part of my life. My degrees are in chemistry, always was in a lab setting in the Air Force. Toward the end, I decided I wanted to teach when I retired, so I took a position at the Air Force Academy, in chemistry, loved it."

He watched her animated hands as she explained getting her teaching credentials, secondary science.

"How the heck did you do that?" Jim shook his head in disbelief.

"Student teacher at a high school right on the Academy grounds, taught chemistry and ran labs with the Academy cadets. For about five months I only slept about four hours a night with that load. The military, they were uber helpful with my future plans."

He watched her smile widen, "Here I am, glad to be here."

"Just two classes and a prep, will you be happy with that?"

"Uh huh," she nodded, "my family's all died early; they're from here. I have land, a corn crop to deal with, and a guy I've loved since forever."

Meredith explained just a little of her relationship with Colin.

"And so you're headed out to new surroundings with your wife, Jim?"

"Right, we're excited; I know I'll find something part time; my love is working with kids and coaching."

"Whew, it's nice that you have a science background."

"Agree."

Meredith gathered the texts and paperwork and put them in her bag. They sat together as he showed her the school's computer she would use.

"I'll bring your kids through the ins and outs of chemistry, Jim. It's good to be a part of something bigger than myself, working with young people," she smiled to him as they shook hands.

"I know you'll do great," she watched his forehead furrow, "bless our students, our future."

It hit her then, just how important her students would become to her.

"Wow, I've got a lot of responsibility. Somehow it weighs on me more than when I taught in the past," she whispered as she walked out of the high school.

She drove out to Landview cemetery and got out to read the guide indicating names and grave locations. Before she walked back to her SUV, she stopped, turning and turning to view a 360 degree sweep of the area, with several tiny hills within her sight.

"These gray graves show up really good with the snowy ground. I honestly do not remember where my family is buried," she shook her head as she drove to the Raymer area. "It was such a hard time for me, so shocking. God, I guess I sorta now understand what your will was for me back then. You wanted me to have a reason to come back to Porttown. I've sure got reasons now, thank you, Lord."

Meredith retrieved three wreaths from the rear of the SUV. She looked again at the crude drawing she made of the area from the legend just inside the graveyard. She trudged along, looking at all the headstones around her.

"I don't recall even being out here for dad's memorial. Was I that much of a mess, with the whole losing him and Conner situation?"

She stopped.

"Yes I was."

Meredith looked to the left and saw the three headstones. She noted with her chemistry eye how the gray granite headstones started to turn black, with the sun and the moisture and the humidity that was outdoor Iowa. Meredith stood in front of her dad's headstone with the three wreaths in her gloved hands.

"First time I've seen your stone, Dad. I just barely got it ordered before I had to get back to my assignment. All I told the stone mason was your vitals and to use the same print style that was on Conner's and Uncle Milt's."

Meredith placed a wreath in front of each of the three head stones and then stepped back. Tears flooded her face; she felt mucous choking her nose and throat.

"I miss you, so much, you three, now that I'm back. Finally I gotta face the fact that you're in my heart and mind and nowhere else," she gasped, shaking her head.

Cold wind pressed against her face as she looked up into the mid-day sun. As she walked back to her SUV, she turned to the right and in her mind she felt the three of them, walking along side of her, and smiling.

℥

Meredith split the next three days into mornings and afternoons. She worked with her lawyer, her CPA, and her insurance advisor in the afternoons. She started coffee at 5:30 a.m., her wakeup time for all her military years, and spent mornings going through her two chemistry textbooks, reviewing lesson plans with the PowerPoint slides. She looked over the practice test for her AP chem students. She found an old file folder with her notes, Prep for AP. She took her finger and skimmed through the information.

"Uh huh, what we worked on, my high school students and me, where I student taught, well I believe I did a good job prepping them for the test."

She nodded as she remembered hearing from her high school mentor teacher later that summer after her student teaching. The majority of her AP students did well on the AP exam.

"So I'll use my same procedures to prep these Porttown High AP kids."

Jess called.

"Hey, I've decided the date when I need to give my AP kids their exam, toward the end of the school year; what's going on with you?"

"I'm on break, before I have to get back to class, Meredith, I need your help."

"What's up?"

"Our church group's run into a snag."

"Tell me what I can do."

"That's exactly what I needed to hear. We're a car short on delivering Christmas boxes to our needy church members. A driver backed out, so there are five boxes."

Meredith stopped her, "When and where?"

Jess filled her in.

"I've got a meeting with my insurance agent. I'll stop by the church meeting hall to get the boxes and my address instructions. Folks should be home by 5:30."

"That's fabulous, Meredith. Here's the number for the woman in charge of the delivery process. She's so worried about everything getting out to our needy."

That evening Meredith spent nearly two hours delivering the boxes. When she left the last family, she could hardly get to her car fast enough. She put her head down the steering wheel and bawled.

"Dear God," she spoke out after her initial crying, "in my own town, folks have desperate situations. That never occurred to me, always on a base, everyone housed in at least a decent place." She raised her head, "But this is the real world, in this the US of A, not a third-world country. These folks, where I've just been, the little kids, God, keep them safe, keep all the families safe."

When Meredith got home, she went straight to her computer to find out the address of the Food Bank in

Porttown. With that information she filled out an envelope and wrote a check.

"There's such a need," she thought as she sealed the envelope for mailing the next day. "I gotta do this often, just like I gotta start contributing to my church. Unbelievable, where've I been, yeah, gone for 20 years, seems like now nobody has enough money. So many folks are just getting by, from meal to meal, paycheck to paycheck.   I think I lived in a pretty sheltered environment."

She picked up her cell and called.

"Hey Jess."

"Yeah, you accomplished the deliveries?"

"Right, oh my gosh, in our own church, folks are having unbelievably hard existences. Is it just living, or have these folks never recovered from the bad years we've had?"

"It's both, Meredith, you're beginning to discover how difficult life is for many folks. You got caught up in your own world, then the Middle East crisis. What's saved you," Jess paused, "and here goes the teacher in me, is that you have a fine education. You've just been shown, by your delivering boxes, what lacking an education can mean."

"Yeah, first hand, walkin' into people's homes, I now, I guess finally realize how important it is, for our young people to have an education. It's a way, to break out of a poverty cycle. So I'm starting to do my part, come January, to be a help with my students' educations. It's the best thing I can do for our Porttown young people."

"You're right, Meredith, our kids are our future."

"Jess, that's so scary, and so exciting, trying to help the kids."

"You're chemistry, so you'll succeed with most students, especially AP, but there are lots."

"Yeah, I know, Jess, lots of kids who need more help, who still want to work out in the world. We still gotta have help in all professions, from our janitors to our doctors to our farm laborers, sorry, I'm blathering."

"Must go, tons to do before I sleep. Let's have lunch."

They set a date and time.

Meredith felt a real unease after her call to Jess.

"What more can I do, what?" she kept asking herself. "Where is this all coming from? Uh huh, the real world just really scares me."

She pondered that, ate soup for supper, and took a pill for her headache. She tumbled into bed early that evening. And in the morning she still settled into a quiet and subdued mood, not like her.

"Colin's coming home, that'll brighten me," she stood, curling her hair in front of the bathroom mirror.

She spent the day going through her notes and the paperwork she got when she visited her lawyer, CPA, and insurance man. After a few hours of study it all started to make sense to her. She owned property which she now would farm, with Colin's help. Her CPA advised her about what to do with profits after all expenses were culled from her budget. He reminded her of the insurance monies which he previously helped her put into the stock market and Roth IRA's. And there was her military retirement, with the benefits that went along with that.

"I'm gonna be OK, money-wise, even if we have a corn failure; I'll still have crop insurance, which'll help some," she reminded herself as she drove to Colin's to spend the night.

They cooked spaghetti together, Colin, the pasta, and Meredith, the sauce from a jar. They both agreed on one brand that tasted great to both of them.

"Not too much garlic, please," Meredith smiled to him.

He stepped forward and took her in his arms, "It'll be OK; we'll have garlicky kisses."

They laughed together, and kissed.

"Pre-garlic breath," Meredith nodded.

He baked the garlic bread in the oven after he slathered on a lot of butter and a little garlic powder on each slice. During dinner he noticed how quiet she was, with him doing all the talking about January and returning to the State House.

"Dear one," he took her hand before they got up from the table, "What's going on, you've not said a word."

"Listening to you, and all you're going to do this session."

"Got to hear from you too."

After they cleaned up, they took their coffee and nearly empty glasses of wine to the couch. Colin started the fire. They sat close, and he put his arm around her shoulder. She turned to him.

"Oh, Colin, oh my gosh, I have so many concerns, kinda scared, so much that's gonna happen. I try to tell myself to take it one day at a time, but it's not working. My mind slogs around like soupy oatmeal."

He hugged her.

"I'm just not the self I was, this civilian role I'm playing. I, I can't even wrap my head around a wedding, that's for starters, after we get the corn planted. My teaching work, that's easy, but wow, everything else."

"Here goes, Meredith, I filed for my slot to seek reelection for state representative in my district. So once again, I'm on my way, have talked to several folks who helped me through the last election. And the wedding, I don't know what you're thinking of. Suggest, maybe, uh, get married in church with Reverend doing the ceremony, have Jess and her new friend stand up with us? That's the important part, our beginning our lives together."

She watched his eyes, intent on her face. He watched a small smile come to her lips.

"Hey, that sounds good, maybe when school's out, early June?"

"Right, the legislative session will be finished; I'll be well into working my reelection, and the corn will be up and doing good, oh and your school year, it'll be finished."

"And then?"

"A reception, here at the farm, Meredith, there're so many people in my life right now. There're my district folks, many who've helped me win the past two elections, and who're on board with me to help me win my third, the many people in our community and our church who've helped me, with contributions and prayers. And oh my gosh, all the farmers in my district, and my constituents at the state capitol. It could end up being a reception for several hundred people. Whadaya think?"

"Yes, I agree. I'm not sure anyone in my military life could attend. They're scattered all over the world."

She sat up tall and straight and turned her head, "But my mom, who I haven't seen in all these years, maybe she would consider coming, Colin, you and me, we have no other family, that's so unbelievable."

"Ask her, Meredith."

She smiled and nodded to him, "Yes, I will. Lots of people will be joyful that you've married. They need to be invited." She paused, "I'll be blunt."

She watched his eyes widen, "Your political career will flourish with me, your wife, by your side."

She saw his smile. They held on to each other, their kisses deepening. Meredith felt the scorch rise from her vagina up and up to her mouth and lips. They helped each other out of their clothes and lay on the rug in front of the fire. He watched her nipples tighten as she gazed up and down his body above her. Seeing his engorged penis brought more fresh liquid to Meredith's wet vagina.

"Want you, Colin."

He eased into her, "I love you, dear one."

They thrust together, riding on a wave of heat, passion.

He burst inside her, "My seed to you."

"I love you," she whispered to him as she shuddered and climaxed.

Later they spooned in his bed.

"Colin?"

"Dear one?"

"I'd like to do at least our first pre-nuptial class with reverend before the end of the year. The more I'm with you the more I realize I don't really know you. I know the surface Colin, like you know me, the surface Meredith. But the 20 years that've passed, we're sorta like blank slates to each other. We must fill in a lot of knowledge, to get to know each other."

"Set it up, Meredith, I agree. In the morning let's sit down together and go over what you've been told by your lawyer and CPA, also your insurance guy. It's critical that we understand each other's finances. A lot of stuff will be in just our own name only, all the land. We may not have that much in joint tenancy."

"Right, now we're talkin' the serious business of marriage."

ℂ

Two afternoons before Christmas Meredith and Colin sat with Reverend Forest in his study. Meredith listened intently to Colin's answers to the reverend's questions as he listened to hers.

"I'm handing you a group of pre-nuptial exercises I want you to do together before I see you again. You've indicated a late spring wedding, right?"

Meredith and Colin both nodded to him.

"So, you haven't said to me, but what about children, planning children?"

Meredith began to shake her head, and Colin followed.

She watched his forehead furrow.

"I haven't even thought about it; we're in the beginnings of getting to know each other sexually after being in love since we were young."

"Right," Meredith agreed. "Reverend, to be honest, we haven't used protection. I'll be 39 in a few days; it never occurred to me, that I could ever even get pregnant, oh dear Lord."

Colin watched Meredith's face blanch to white.

He took her hand, "Do you think, is it possible?"

She shook her head to him, "Don't know." She turned to the minister, "Sorry Reverend, you've gotten too much intimate detail. Wow, oh my gosh."

Reverend Forest smiled to them both, "Passion's overtaken reason."

Reverend watched Meredith and Colin nod to each other. Colin took Meredith's hand and held it.

"Switching gears, your legislative session begins soon, Colin?"

"Yes, after the first of the year; I'll be in Des Moines, and getting back here to be with Meredith on weekends when I can."

"And you, Meredith?"

She went on to tell him about working with students in chemistry at Porttown High.

"I'm excited; my students in our community, together, all of us, must prepare them for the world they're stepping into."   She nodded her head and smiled first to the reverend and then to Colin, "They're our future."

They stood and thanked him, then shook hands with Reverend Forest.

"You both are in my thoughts and in my prayers; enormous responsibilities are being placed on your shoulders. And Colin, we thank you for your service to our church as a deacon. Other duties call you now."

Meredith heard the serious tone of his voice as he finished, "God bless and keep you."

They held hands as they walked toward their cars. Colin stopped her at her car.

"We have so much to ponder, our future, together."

Meredith looked up into his eyes, "So serious, what we face."

They hugged.

"Wanta join Jess and me for the 9 p.m. service, Christmas eve?"

He held her tighter.

"That's tomorrow night, yes I can make it.   And Christmas day?"

"Jess asked us both to join her and her friend at noon for a meal and games later."

They stepped away from each other.

"It's what we need, after this mind-bending time with our minister."

"Right, Colin, that was some serious stuff in there with him. We have to get to know each other again, we love, but, do you like me?"

He smiled down to her and kissed her on top of her head, "Yes, dear one, I like you."

"You are my best friend, Colin."

"And you like me?"

"I do."

As Meredith drove toward her home, she tried to gather her scattered thoughts.

"One day, Meredith, just this day, it's precious."

She took deep breaths and by the time she reached her apartment she felt more in control.

℣

Colin and Meredith picked Jess up for the Christmas Eve celebration at church. All through the service Meredith noted how well the choir sang, joyous voices for this holiday season, with the congregation adding their singing to this special occasion of Christ's birth.

"I'm happy to be home, with my family, I really am," she decided as she looked to Colin and then turned to Jess. "Thank you God, for how Your will's helped me."

Colin spent the night with Meredith. She bounded from bed at 5:30 a.m. and looked into the dark outdoors to glimpse a covering of snow on the ground. At breakfast they each shared about a past Christmas in their lives, one which the other person wouldn't have known about. Meredith turned on the Christmas lights as they sat together on the loveseat. They already bought each other a present, but Colin wanted them to wrap them, and open gifts on Christmas morning.

"Exactly, I like the color you picked, the light blue, Meredith, I gave you a couple of choices."

"It's wrinkle resistant, you especially asked for that in the shirt."

"And the tie, perfect, you picked it out by yourself."

"I did, keeping in mind how you'd look to your many constituents where you work."

Colin handed Meredith her gift. A few days before they did their shopping together. Meredith saw three different bracelets she liked. But she told Colin he would need to decide, to make it a sort of surprise.

Now she unwrapped the box and gazed at the bracelet.

She gasped, "Oh my gosh, Colin, it's so beautiful."

He put it on her wrist, "You sure don't wear jewelry, except your ears."

"But this, I'll wear, and treasure this wonderful diamond bracelet, thank you, Colin."

He took her in his arms and whispered, "It's important to me that you have it; you requested no engagement ring."

"And next Christmas, we'll be together, in front of the fire in our home in the country."

"Our dreams keep unfolding, Meredith."

℥

"What're we supposed to bring?"

"Jess wanted me to pick a special wine, that goes with ham, so this guy's one I picked up in Turkey."

"Wow, that should taste pretty special."

"We'll see; I bought two bottles, haven't tried it yet. It'll be a grand experiment."

After they settled in at Jess's, Meredith handed her the envelope.

"I gave you several ideas," she smiled to Meredith, "let's see what you decided," as she tore open the envelope.

She read through the information and came to hug Meredith.

"Awesome, a perfect Christmas present."

Jess handed the paperwork to Colin.

"A massage?" he raised his eyebrows and shook his head.

"Hey, I like being pampered, whenever I can be."

"Jess told me dad gave her a massage gift certificate every year."

"That's right, he took very good care of me," she spoke with a choked voice. They watched tears come to her eyes.

"Oh, you two, finally I can say it, Jack," she stopped as her tears continued, "I really feel died of a broken heart, two of the people he cared most about, his brother, and his son, gone, Conner just a few days before. Jack wanted to be with them more than he wanted to stay alive, that's it, that's what I feel, his heart, it just let go, so he could be with them, and with his God."

"Oh my gosh, ladies, new revelations about each of you just keep coming to me."

Jess laughed through her tears as she turned to give Colin a hug.

"So, before my guest arrives, he's Sam Justine, and we met each other helping to organize our church's family gift boxes."

Jess gazed at Colin as the guest's name registered with him.

"Meredith, does that name sound familiar to you?"

"Ooohhh, not so much, I've met some folks since I've been back."

Colin looked at Jess, "Ah yeah, this will be an interesting meal. Sam is your boss, Meredith."

He watched Meredith shake her head and give him her googly eyes.

"He's Porttown High's principal."

"OK," she swallowed hard, "and you've been seeing him?"

"Off and on since last Christmas," Jess smiled, "he's widowed, three years, kids raised, no grandkids yet. I really like him."

"Gosh, that's wonderful, Jess, no conflict of interest, since you're at an elementary school, Colin, did you know?"

Colin smiled, nodding to Meredith and Jess. Meredith filtered through the little information she remembered from her interview with the principal and the head of the science department at Porttown High. She couldn't remember a single question he asked her.

"Everything's delicious, Jess," Meredith touched her arm.

"Here, here," Sam nodded his head as he smiled to Jess.

Meredith saw it, and so did Colin. They could both feel the affection Jess and Sam had as they ate the meal.

"Their eyes, on each other, a special caring," Meredith mused.

The wine from Turkey tasted tart, with a hint of cherry. Meredith shared her story of bartering for it in a Turkish market.

Sam and Colin carried the conversation, through dinner, coffee and dessert.

"Ain't no secret," Sam drawled and continued, "I voted for you twice, Colin, and I'll vote for you again. But next time, in '14, let's see about vacancies in our state area, for US House of Representatives. You'll have a shot at that, with six years experience under your belt."

Colin gave him a thumbs up, "Thanks for your confidence."

Colin gazed at Meredith, remembering how she talked about helping him to some day get to that US Rep spot. Meredith sat, remembering the same conversation and smiling to Colin.

"So Colin," Jess asked, "what's on the legislative agenda for '12?"

"Economic growth, taxpayers controlling growth of property taxes, and voluntary soil and water conservation improvement programs for starters."

"Which one for you?" Sam asked.

"With my ag background it'll be working the soil/water effort. A couple of Iowa State profs will be helping me with the natural resource background info we'll need. The key is that everything'll be voluntary, in what our farmers and ranchers decide to do. Hey, 'nuf about me."

"And you, Meredith, I remember from your resume and talking to a reference, that you're really into chemistry."

Meredith acknowledged Sam, "National defense, weapons, terrorism in the war, most of what I did is classified, so can't ever talk about it. I went into the Air Force hoping to do some good for our country. I'm proud of my efforts to help out. For now, I'll educate our students in chemistry. The AP chemistry kids, well they'll really be neat to work with. All our young people," she held her hands out, "our future."

"Amen to that," Sam nodded.

&

He heard the knock.

"It's unlocked," she heard him holler from somewhere inside.

Meredith grasped the doorknob with one hand and picked up her clothing bag with the other. She let herself in and set the bag down. Just as she got her boots off, Colin came to greet her.

They hugged.

"Such a nice Christmas day."

"You made it very special, Meredith."

"All packed?"

"Course, always prepared," she kissed him and he kissed her back.

As they agreed, Meredith moved her SUV to a parking spot inside Colin's large three-car garage.

"Jess sent leftovers from Christmas dinner. Let's have those before long. I want a nice fire, a little wine, and you by my side on this Christmas night."

"Awesome, I'm headed up to the bedroom, to get stuff out for tonight. Anything I can do to help?"

"Nah, got it under control, bring down your pre-nup stuff. I got mine. And let's share before early dinner. I want to get out of here early tomorrow. There's lots I want to show you."

Colin poured wine and they sat together at the large kitchen island.

"Hey, this isn't very Christmasy, but it's us, it's important, it's the rest of our lives."

As Reverend Forest asked, they exchanged information they wrote out at an earlier time. On page one each wrote a description of self. On page two each wrote expectations they had of the other person. Page three addressed money issues and children. On page four each wrote out dreams for the future, for each of them, and for them together.

"Toughest writing assignment I've ever had," Colin blew out a breath as he nodded his head to Meredith.

"For sure," she agreed.

Two hours later they finished going through the thoughts they wrote.

"Hey, I'm starving, but this is helping me so much, to get to know you, Colin, I just feel like I'm maybe, just beginning to know who you really are."

"Same, oh my gosh, same for me, we'll save this, to discuss with the reverend the next time we meet."

They hummed a Christmas melody playing in the background as they took their plates of food and ate by the fire in the great room. Meredith poured more wine, and they shared the big piece of apple pie.

"So cinammony, the crust super flakey, wow," they nodded to each other.

Later, after they made love, Colin moved his ear to her heart.

"Your heartbeat, so quiet, it sounds like a whisper."

Meredith moved to his beating heart, "Yours is a little louder, but maybe a whisper compared to the pound, pound when our hearts race, when we thrust so deep."

"Quiet, like now."

"Our heartbeats, a whisper, a whisper song, that's us, Colin, we have a whisper song."

"Like that, Meredith, I do."

He gathered her in his arms as they fell asleep.

☙

Meredith went directly to the window after she awoke.

"No new snow, yay, it'll be an easy drive to Des Moines."

"Come back to bed, oh wide awake one."

"Happy day after Christmas, oh, I love you, Colin."

She burrowed back into the cozy warm bed and spooned into Colin's chest and legs.

"And I love you, Meredith, stay with me for just a moment, I gotta savor this, for all my mornings when you'll not be with me."

She flipped around and hugged him, giving him a big kiss on the lips and then a kiss on each side of his face.

"Are you thoroughly awake, my representative man?"

"I am, join me in the shower?"

"Uh huh, but I take fast showers; I'll show you how."

Meredith scrubbed him down with soap and water, and he did the same with her.

"Quick, quick, Colin, a fast soap removal, turn, turn, now turn me."

"Stop, I need a hug, before we step out."

Meredith started laughing, "The funny guy, always needing his hugs at the darndest times."

"Hey, that was great play time, and we got washed to boot," Colin joined in laughing.

They dried off, using the thick, wonderful smelling towels.

"So that's it, the quick shower."

"Uh huh, Colin, take time off for the hug, that made it pretty quick."

"Your shower style, all through the military?"

"Yeah."

"Hope you stand in the shower now, and take a moment to savor the warmth."

"I do, but I try not to waste water."

Colin moved his arms around her, "Dear one, you are really somethin' else."

"Uh, huh," she stood on her tiptoes and kissed him on the mouth.

"I'd return the kiss, but we gotta head out."

ℰℭ

"Oh Colin, what a magnificent structure."

He walked with Meredith around the entire outside of the Iowa capitol. That way she could see the five domes that he talked about. She stopped and gazed up at the main dome.

"It's pretty amazing, so golden, shining in the sunlight."

"Wait'll I take you inside; you'll be able to look straight up to the top of the dome. Would you like to walk up to it?"

"Yes, of course."

They held hands as they walked around in the main rotunda of the building and up and up the steps to view the ceiling of the dome.

"Could spend a lot of time, observing everything that's here."

"One day I want you to come and take a guided tour, and look in on the senate and house chambers. Tour's helpful, so much wonderful info, the history, architecture. Hey, there's one place you need to see."

After 15 minutes of viewing the room Meredith whispered, "Wow, Colin, this for sure is my favorite."

"It is for many folks; they like the library most over all the other chambers in the building. Maybe it's the sheer number of books, the quiet, it's a wondrous place for me. I come here, once in a while," he paused, "to think."

"Just awesome, Colin," she tiptoed, giving him a kiss.

"My political world, Meredith, whatcha think?"

"You represent us Iowa folks, from our area, thank you for showing me what your world will look like for the next few months."

He took her to his office. She noticed his orderly desk and computer area.

"You have a work table, nice, for projects."

She touched the surface of a dark circle table. It had four matching chairs with dark green upholstered seats.

"Bet some decisions get made around this table, Colin."

"That's right, at various times committees break down into small groups. There've been a few 2 a.m. sessions around this guy."

"Now I see why you keep a reserve coffee maker next to the one you usually use. And I bet a few times you've slept on this couch in your office."

"Guilty, keep extra shirts here too."

"For the long grueling days toward the end of April?"

"Correct, when the legislature's just gotta get everything acted on for recess."

"Back to your place?"

"Uh huh, I want you to see where I stay; maybe you can visit sometime, spend a Saturday night with me when issues start rushing at us."

"Yeah, instead of you always having to come back to Porttown."

"Right."

They walked hand in hand, Colin pointing out places she might want to know about on the way to the apartment.

"You really walk fast, Meredith, that's the discipline I see never leaving you."

"Uh huh, my early years in the military, there was a lot more walking, parading, show stuff, than later on less, as I moved up the ranks. Being in a laboratory setting all the time gave us all more of a science mode than a military mode."

"For sure, you'll always have that military bearing, Meredith, the straight back, eyes forward, hey, that's a compliment."

She turned to him and put her hand on his shoulder as they stopped walking.

"And I thank you for that," she widened her smile as she touched his cheek.

Meredith glanced around his apartment living room, but what caught her eye was a photo, very enlarged, in black and white. She stepped closer, and gasped.

"That me?" she spoke out.

"Uh huh, I snapped that when you were at our old place, pulling deadheads from Mom's roses."

"I don't remember that, at all, the summer dad asked me to come home to help out after mom left us?"

"Yeah, that summer, the shot captured your fabulous wide smile, which you still have. Meredith, it's my favorite of you."

He stepped close and took her in his arms, "I still can't believe it; here you are with me, here in Des Moines."

"I'm so glad we came, to help me see your complete world."

On the kitchen counter she saw a note, addressed to Colin. She handed it to him.

He laughed after he opened the paper up and read the note.

"My apartment mate, he's already been here, getting ready for the session."

He handed the note to Meredith.

> Holy crap, Colin, glad you said something about having your lady visit our apartment, a lieutenant colonel, oh my gosh, golly, shit, I hope the place will meet with her approval. I didn't touch your room, which is always shipshape. But I had to work in my room, to clear clutter, also in the living room. Looking forward to seeing you soon. And thanks for the e-mail about Meredith. Beer in frig, yay. JJC

"OK, he sounds like a character."

"Oh man, he is, about all we keep in the frig is beer, eat out most of the time."

"That sounds expensive."

"Nah, not really, eat a lot at the capitol, and places nearby. Nothin's close, groceries, all that stuff, so I bring from home when I can. I'm just so glad we have laundry facilities in our apartment complex."

They continued standing in the kitchen.

She touched his arm, "Colin, do you remember, when you lost your family, how you talked about hating laundry, doing it only when it piled so high."

"Yeah, I remember," he put his arm around her shoulder, "I'm better now, wash my sheets more often, and keep a week's worth of clean shirts in the closet. That's why I asked for a wrinkle-free shirt from you for Christmas. Hey, and I brought it along to add to my collection."

They helped each other bring in their bags from the SUV Colin drove. She put her small bag in the far corner of his bedroom. She glimpsed the earth tones of his drapes, the pale green of his bedspread, and the brown towels hanging in his bathroom.

"Colin, this room, it's so what you are, the brown of the soil, the green of the corn plants as they rise from the ground."

"Yeah, it's a calming room, which I need after some of our sessions, unbelievable the decisions we have to make, that affect all the people of Iowa. It scares me sometimes, what I have to do, for now, what we need to do, ahead, to our future, our state's future."

Meredith nodded and smiled to him.

"Hey, I'll let you freshen up. I gotta get into my e-mail. Then let's walk to an early dinner; there's a place I like, want you to see.

Meredith helped herself to a beer and put a beer for Colin on a table near the computer. He insisted on no liquid near his computer or that area. She closed her eyes as she sat in the comfy chair.

"Oh my dear one, my sleepy head, I thought you should rest a bit," he kissed her on the top of her head.

Meredith roused, "Crashed, man, all the excitement of seeing your world."

They went to dinner and returned to the apartment.

"First time."

"Huh, first time?"

"Meredith, this is the first time I've made love in this bed. All these years, there was no one I wanted but you. So bed, you've been initiated."

Meredith laughed and laughed at his solemn remarks directed to the bed where they would spend the rest of the night.

"That's a lot of information you just gave me, uh, and the bed."

"It's the truth, dear one, and I'm so happy you're here with me."

They clung to each other as sleep enfolded them.

⁊

Meredith got permission to spend three days of the week after Christmas at Porttown High. She received keys, to her room, chem lab, and supply room. As was her habit in first starting a lab assignment, she took an inventory for everything necessary for her students to complete the lab assignments that would occur during the semester. By first thing the morning of the second day, she took a list of chemicals and equipment she needed to the secretary who handled that process.

"We'll order these by phone to our suppliers. That'll be the fastest way to get what you need. Your stuff should be here within a week. Now that the holidays are over the mail service gets really efficient again. Should'a asked first, but Meredith, did you clear this with our science department head?" Jan asked.

"Uh huh, he's surprised and happy that I did an inventory. I guess they didn't even think about it with Jim leaving. I want a smooth transition for both me and the students who'll have me as an instructor. Thank you for taking care of this for me; you're covering for all the staff this week."

"I am, it's my pleasure to help you out; we're all here for our students, Meredith. You're our newcomer, our newest faculty member, helping us help our kids."

Jan watched Meredith smile and nod to her.

"For the kids," Meredith mouthed as she walked back to her classroom and lab.

When she returned to the lab, she looked through one of the bags she brought from home.

"Here you are, old favorite lab coat, all clean."

Meredith shook it out and hung it on the hook she found in the supply closet.

She touched the coat, "We've been a lot of places together, old favorite friend. But we got more adventures, right?"

Meredith shook her head, "Anybody watching me must think I'm crazy, talkin' to a coat!"

She spent a few more minutes in the lab, remembering the first aid kit and the eye rinse equipment she needed to put away in a safe area of the lab. She thought ahead to her first lab lecture with Porttown students, the same one she did wherever she was in charge of a lab. From her first lab, back 20 years ago, the safety first aspect of everything that needed to happen was always her primary objective.

Meredith locked her classroom door. She felt her cellphone vibrate in her pocket. She stood in the hall and answered it.

"Hey, dear one, you know what day today is?"

3

"Wow, I hadn't even thought about it. I missed so many of these days in the past."

"Happy Birthday, Meredith, the last one of your 30's. OK if I come over about 5? I got stuff to do with you."

"Oh, you do?"

"Yeah, see you then."

Meredith took a mental inventory a few minutes before Colin arrived. She ticked off laundry, groceries, cleaning her apartment, going to her safety deposit box to retrieve documents and put others back, and being ready for her first day of classes.

"Gosh, water the tree," she spoke out as she grabbed a small pitcher. After she poured the water in the stand, she felt the fir needles on several places of the tree.

"Still moist, yay, little tree, you'll be up for a while."

She gazed at her French horn in its case and the music stand with music she wanted to play. She picked up the music on the stand.

"I can't wait to get back to my music, with the symphony, uh, if they'll let me in the group after all this time; I'll need to practice and then try out."

She heard Colin's knock on her door.

They exchanged hugs and a long, deep kiss. She stepped back from him as he noted her red sweater and black slacks.

"Hey, what you're wearing's great; we have a couple of stops this evening, that is, stuff connected with celebrating a birthday," he gave her a lazy grin and winked.

&

"It's midnight, that was so fun, Colin, meeting up with those two couples for an early meal. Gosh, they're friendly, accepted me like they'd known me all my life."

"Yeah, that's the way the Cowden's and Apperson's are. Those guys, and their wives, huge supporters of me all through my legislative time. I went to school with Adam Cowden, both at Porttown High and then Iowa State."

"That was a great country band, Colin, I don't remember dancing with you back in the day. You had so much fun, and teaching me that line dance. I been out of touch for a long time, with a lot of things."

"We'll catch you up, but now, we gotta eat cake. It sat in the backseat of my car for long enough, vanilla ice cream?"

"'Course, dessert stuff is high on my food agenda."

They ate together, sitting on the love seat, still hearing Christmas music from CD's.

"The tree's staying lovely, Meredith. You're gonna keep it up a while, right?

"Uh huh, I love Christmas, it goes on and on for me. It's to make up for all the years when I just wasn't around for the holidays. Hey, when the decorations finally come down, I will, for the rest of the year, sing, 'Christmas is coming', to *Silent Night*."

They slept in the next morning. Meredith tiptoed out in her bare feet to get the newspaper.

"That was pretty dumb, Meredith," she chided herself, "you'll get sick and have a cold for your first days of class, dumb, dumb."

She found the socks she should have worn when she went outside and put them on her freezing feet. In the kitchen she made coffee and turned on her National Public Radio station. As she sipped the brew, she felt a large presence behind her.

"You're up. I let you sleep, thought you needed to."

He kissed the top of her head. She set the cup down and turned around to him. She saw he wore his holey Iowa State t-shirt and wrinkled blue plaid boxer shorts.

"Don't matter what you got on, Colin Sanderson, you look plenty wonnerful to me."

He stepped back and bowed to her, "So pleased you approve, madam," in his clipped British accent.

They both broke into laughter. Then Meredith bowed to him. She wore her ancient Air Force ROTC t-shirt and shorts, from physical training all those years ago.

"We sure do love our old stuff."

"Yeah, it's soft and comfortable."

They came together and kissed, a soft caressing kiss.

"Breakfast coming up."

"Good, I'm starved, Meredith. You cook good bacon and eggs."

"Birthday cake, first, OK?"

"Yeah, dessert first, this cake is delicious, Colin."

"Uh huh, the store has super good bakery stuff, always has."

They proceeded to down the bacon, eggs and toast. Meredith drank her third cup of coffee.

"Plans for New's Year's Eve?"

"None, just be with you if I can be."

"I want to take you to the New Year's Eve dance at the country club."

They sat close together at the small table.

"To dance again with you, that'd be super special. Colin, you're not even gone yet, and I'm missing not being with you. All these years, I've missed you, our times together from now on are gonna be real precious."

"For sure, precious, and it'll be good to see how we do, for the next few months, while I'm in Des Moines and you're here."

"Well, I'm super independent, and so are you, from our many years of being single. We'll be just fine."

℘

Meredith's head swirled by 11 p.m. on New Year's Eve. Colin must have introduced her to at least 70 people while they danced and mingled with the crowd.

"Everyone seems so pleased, so surprised, as you introduce me as your fiancé, Colin."

"Yeah, I didn't tell anyone what's been on my mind, until now."

He held her close as they danced a slow dance.

"You look stunning tonight, Meredith, a bright light in your eyes."

"So you approve of my black gown; it's pretty modest."

"Yeah, well I sure as heck do approve. It shows off your slim figure to perfection. Guess I'm real old fashioned, but I like to think that seeing breasts is reserved only for the man who loves his woman."

She lifted her head up and looked into his eyes, "I sure do love you, Colin."

"And I love you, Meredith."

They sat for a few minutes. More folks stopped by, and Colin made introductions. Meredith gazed around at the lovely table settings and the happy couples talking and dancing.

"This is a part of my world now, the social part, that Colin must do," she thought. Her eyes wandered to the couples on the dance floor. "Colin, wanna try the line dance."

"Sure."

While they were out on the floor, in the middle of a song, the music stopped. The whole room helped count down to 2012. Colin picked Meredith up and held her as they turned completely around.

"Happy New Year, dear one."

"And Happy New Year to you."

They kissed. Face to face he held her tight against him. He set her down in a gentle gesture.

&

At the end of her first week of teaching Meredith started to feel confident in the chemistry she taught in her classroom with her students, and in her lab. She began lab instruction on the third day of classes and she told her students about her chemistry background and what little she could about her mission throughout her time in the Air Force. Her lab remained her comfort zone, as she expressed to them.

She and Colin kept in touch by e-mail. His work at the state house roared ahead. It looked like he might be able to break away, after he put in two full weeks. Already he worked very long days, going in early and staying late. He mentioned to her several times how much more comfortable he felt in this second year of his second term, like he finally belonged with the legislature.

"The weather's terrible; I'm staying put and working on my latest project, Meredith. I'll try to get home next Friday night."

"Fer sure I don't want you traveling home in adverse conditions. I'll be fine; I always got school work. I'm also making my plan for the corn planting. Your part-time helper, he's already consented to helping me out with the planting. We'll get'er all done, my corn and yours."

"You two discussed the corn type, based on the pest problems we've had the last two years?"

"I have, and the corn seeds are on order. He and I are gonna do a section of one of my fields in a special drought-resistant corn seed. Yeah, I know, I know, we get lots of rain here, but I just want to do an experiment, kinda like what the kids and I do in chem lab, course the seeds are long term, not like our short 20 minute experiments."

"Soy beans?"

"Right, in between the fields of corn, that's kinda another practice I hadn't heard much about."

ঞ

Reverend Forest completed his sermon. For some reason, as Meredith sat in church that Sunday, what he had to say about responsibility brought up her personal calendar. Church concluded, and she greeted folks outside. A plan formed in her mind.

"Get to the drug store; find out what's going on."

She noticed the tingling feeling in her breasts as she put on her lab coat a few days before. She lifted up her arms as she swung the lab coat through her left arm and around to her right arm. When she got home, she examined her breasts in the bathroom lights. She saw the darkening of her nipples. She never remembered that before. And she had not had a period since before Thanksgiving.

Now here she stood, a few days later at the bathroom sink, with a pregnancy test held with the fingers of her left hand. She did the test again, a second test. The results remained the same. Meredith examined her personal calendar, from last year, and her calendar for 2012.

Sweat formed on her forehead. She wiped it away with the back of her hand.

"Dear God, what have I done?" she paused, "no, what have we done, Colin and me?"

After a series of calls, she received the name of an OBGYN in her area that her retiree military medical benefits would certify. She called, getting an appointment several days later because of the nature of her situation.

ঞ

"I'm pleased, that you are seeing me now. Meredith, as soon as it's possible, I'll run tests, including an amniocentesis, to help determine the condition of the fetus. Let's get information about your family."

"My brother, Conner, had Down Syndrome."

Meredith began to choke, remembering her dear brother.

"He, he lived a good life, lived longer than anyone anticipated, a happy, contented man. My Uncle Milt, my dad's brother, had borderline mental retardation. He helped on the farm, and he had a good life, happy just like my brother. Nobody before my uncle or brother, that we knew of, had any mental retardation, not anybody in our family, for as far back as my parents, well."

Meredith stopped talking, shaking her head and breaking into tears.

"Your parents, Meredith?"

"Dad died in 2005, two weeks after my brother, Conner died."

"Mom?"

"Lives in California, divorced from my dad for a long time. I haven't seen her since I was 16. She walked away from my dad. When that happened my dad requested that I come home from college. They were all pretty devastated. I helped everyone until they got on their feet, gone from school over a summer and a semester. Then I returned to K State and came back for a few days before my graduation. I didn't return until I lost my dad and brother. I'm retired from the Air Force, 20 years, lieutenant colonel."

"What field?"

"Chemistry, lab situation, intense after 911."

"Oh my goodness, is this a surprise?"

"Uh, more like an absolute shock, my guy and I took no precautions, he's mid-forties. It just didn't occur to us, that at our age, we could," Meredith's eyes widened, "well, have this happen."

"Married to him?"

"No, we're in the beginning stages of planning a June wedding, just went to our first pre-nup session with Reverend Forest from our church. Then we sat down and wrote out the assignment he gave us. On the page about family and children, we just both put down a big question mark."

"Go on."

"Dear God, I just don't know what to do. I'm a chemistry teacher, part time at Porttown High. Colin Sanderson, my guy, is."

Dr. Farley interjected, "One of our state representatives, from our district. He's in session now?"

"Right."

"I voted for him."

Meredith managed a small smile and nod.

"I can tell, by watching your face and your demeanor, that this is pretty upsetting for you."

"Upsetting isn't the word, I, I," Meredith stopped and blew out a breath, "I feel like I've been hit by a truck. I sure as hell need your advice."

Her eyes bored into the doctor's eyes.

"I see some anger in your eyes, they're a lot darker than when we began chatting. Since you're older, you're a special case, especially with the family history you have. I'll watch over you with extra care. Do you love the father of your child?"

"Oh my gosh, oh yes, I love him with all my heart, been in love since my college days, but it's just been since I retired from the Air Force that our lives came together. We communicated once a year, Christmas cards, for the 20 years we were apart. I moved back to Porttown to take over my family's farm, and to work with students in chemistry."

"That's quite a history."

"I was just getting my civilian life in order, getting used to the new me, and now this, as I asked before," she paused, "advice."

"Friends here, I know you're new, returning, 20 years away?"

"One female friend, the best, and of course, Colin."

"Your decision, tell your guy, for sure, and your concern about your family history. You two will need to decide about the baby, especially if the abnormalities in the fetus show up."

"Uh huh, also, oh my gosh, we're now in the public eye, get married sooner."

"Up to you, Meredith, but that sounds appropriate."

"What have I done, oh what have I done? I'm like the 16 year old who got caught, no protection with her guy, had to get married, geez I used to talk about loose girls like that. Hey I'm no better than her."

The doctor touched Meredith's arm, "Get your attitude around the love of a child."

"I think I'm gonna be sick."

Meredith put her head down between her legs and began gagging. She held her stomach and began taking deep breaths, in and out, like in the old days, when she helped her fellow officers through physical training.

"Don't beat yourself up, Meredith, you can call this a mistake, or you can call it a blessing."

Meredith raised her head, took her hands away from her stomach and rested for a moment.

"Yeah, I know, just hit me, God's in charge, guess this is what he wants for us, Colin and me. I know He doesn't want me to abort, each of us, everyone, is a child of God, regardless."

"We'll hope for the most positive outcome from your tests. You are in especially good health, from your background and your continual attention to physical training. And your guy, in good health?

"Yes."

Doctor Farley saw a wide smile form on Meredith's face as she nodded.

"I'm writing out a prescription of the standard vitamins I ask all my patients to begin taking. Folic acid, as in way back in the day, when you were born, is an essential component of the vitamins you'll take. What was the age difference between you and your brother?"

"18 months, exactly, I'm the younger. My folks raised us pretty much as twins, walked and talked about the same time."

"I'll bet you are one reason your brother did so well with his situation, he had a very smart sister, to help him along."

Meredith nodded her head to the doctor and then gazed above her, remembering past days, "I, I guess that's right, hey, and love, we loved each other very much, Conner and me."

"Let's see you in three weeks, that'll put you at the ninth week or so, then we'll decide when to do the tests, morning sickness, tired at night?"

"Not so far, that's why this is so unbelievable, except for the color of my breast nipples," she giggled.

The doctor laughed, "So far, so good."

℃

Jess saw the tears in Meredith's eyes as soon as she walked in the door. They hugged.

"Decaf coffee?

"Yeah, I really need the caffeine, but I gotta sleep tonight, so I'll go for the taste."

They sat across from each other at the kitchen table, sipping their coffee. Jess waited, knowing Meredith filtered her thought process.

Meredith mopped her face and blew her nose.

She shook her head to Jess, "You gotta swear to keep this to yourself. I'm, I'm pregnant," she paused, "pregnant, and not married. Our passion for each other just ruled out everything else, wanting to be together, wanting to connect, to become one. Reverend Forest mentioned something about passion overtaking reason, when we had our first pre-nup talk with him."

Meredith drained her cup, got up and refilled it from the pot nearby.

"What now?" Jess raised her eyebrows to Meredith.

"That's why I'm here, for your advice. Me, who used to help make decisions impacting our country, our national security. I feel like a blithering idiot right now, way out of my comfort zone."

"OK, hear me out, and no interruptions, please," Jess spoke to Meredith in her strong teacher voice, as if addressing a class full of squirmy youngsters.

"Tell Colin now. You and he decide about the amniocentesis, which you must have, with your family background, and then you go from there. He's a very visible face; you plan to marry in June, perhaps move the date up, to say next month. Have you told anyone else about your June plans?"

"Nope," Meredith shook her head.

"If you want, I can help you with planning; since you and he've both been married before, and given he's at the capitol most of the time until May, and you're here. A simple ceremony and do some sort of reception, baby, August?"

Meredith nodded, then put her head down on the table and whispered the *Lord's Prayer*, Jess joining in to help her finish the prayer. She raised her head and wiped tears from her face.

"I heard what you said and that all sounds really good. That really helps me."

She downed the coffee and got herself a final half cup.

"My addiction," she nodded to Jess.

Meredith continued to stand; it helped contain the sparks of energy that jumped around inside her body. She felt a real unease about herself.

"It's all gonna work out, Meredith, remember, God's."

"In charge, I must think about that every time I start to worry. I love Colin so much. I should be so happy right now."

"It'll come, face forward and get going on all the things you must do."

ℰℐ

"I'm so glad to be home; it's been crazy, so many bills the Iowa house is introducing, need to get back Sunday afternoon. Should I come to you?"

"Excellent, I'll do lasagna and pick a dessert. I love you, Colin and I've missed you."

"Love you, I'll get stuff done and see you about 7."

Meredith set her cell down and pulled the lasagna from the freezer. After she put the frozen container in the heated oven, she looked over the notes she took when she got home from Jess's the night they talked.

She stood in the shower and hollered, "I'm scared, I'm afraid, I'm scared, shitless, outa my mind."

Later, as she put the finishing touches on the meal, a calm, like a soothing blanket, wrapped around her.

"Maybe I should just shout out once in a while, it seemed to help me," she thought.

They stood together in her kitchen. Colin poured them wine.

"Hey, I been doin' all the talking; I want to know about your week, your students, school, the crop plans."

Meredith took a tiny sip of her wine. She touched Colin's shoulder as he turned to her.

"Colin," she looked up into his eyes, "I'm pregnant."

He took her wine glass and set it down beside his. She saw his smile and his shining blue eyes. He gathered her in his arms as she reached up to enclose him in hers. They held on to each other for a very long time, the silence broken by the clicking of the oven timer.

"A baby, we've made a baby, a gift from God, oh Meredith, that's fabulous, oh, I'm in shock, I, I didn't know if I could, well, oh I love you, Meredith."

They held on to each other for a little while longer.

"I love you, Colin."

℘

"Wondrous lovemaking tonight with you, Meredith, you're my precious dear one, each time we're together, it's magic. What we feel, it just grows and grows," he said as they lay together on her bed, the covers all in a jumble.

"Yes, wondrous, but Colin, I'm scared, so much facing us ahead."

She burrowed into his neck and chest as he stroked her back.

"I feel positive, every confidence that all will work out. Be happy, Meredith, I am so happy for me, for you, for us.

The amniocentesis, it'll be essential, and the other tests your doctor can do. Does anyone know your situation?"

"Only Jess, and my doctor, that's the way I want to keep it, no one else. It'll be the tests, yes, the tests."

Colin leaned on his right elbow and touched her cheek with his left hand.

"You're fearful, you're uncertain, I can understand that. You're no longer in your safe, military place. I felt like you do now, my first term at the state house. But you know what?"

"What?"

"In a real slow fashion my fear, it got replaced with faith, faith in my efforts, individually and group. Our bills got passed; changes were made in laws. Soon I got confidence, to replace my uncertainty. Faith, in God, in yourself, it'll replace fear. Confidence, from God and from the inner strong person that you are, will replace your uncertainty."

"I'm listening, oh Colin I hope that is the case for me."

"It will be. We need to sleep. In the morning we will plan our future, dear one."

"Our future," Meredith caressed his lips with her own as they lay together, "our future."

₧

Meredith joined the Porttown Symphony. Practicing at home and with the symphony once a week brought her a musical joy that she missed over all the years in the military.

"It's a fill-in position for a woman with a baby coming very soon. Will that work for you, Meredith?" the symphony conductor asked. "We really need you through the end of the school year."

"That works out fine; I've other plans after I complete my year at Porttown High. You all take a break for the summer."

He nodded his head to her and smiled, "Every few years we decide to do something for the 4th of July; it's always special, but simple."

"It's a pleasure to get back to my French horn and help you out. Music calms me, yours is a heavenly symphony."

"Why thank you, that's a touching gesture, Meredith."

They shook hands. Meredith felt a bounce in her step as she carried her French horn case from the practice hall out into the snowy night.

∾

"I love you, Meredith, before I head to my bed here in Des Moines and you, your Porttown bed, update me, dear one."

"Hope it's gonna work for you, Colin. Actually I'm having fun with this, 'cause Jess is helping."

Colin waited for her to go on.

"Exchange vows with Reverend Forest Saturday morning, February 11th at 9:30 in the church and have Jess and Sam as our witnesses. It'll be the four of us."

"Great."

"The invitations go out tomorrow, for our welcoming reception from one to four p.m. that afternoon at your home. You're sure about the location?"

"Positive, I want everyone to meet you, see our home (it's OUR home, Meredith), our sanctuary of love."

"Caterers, with their helpers, they'll mingle with finger foods, cake and champagne, and coffee, and punch for little people. Caterer's taking care of outside helpers who'll make certain cars get parked. If necessary a landscape crew will plow Saturday morning to clear snow away. People will be parking only on the lane coming in, and outside along the paved county road."

"Hey, that's some organized caterer."

"Well, Colin, I feel pretty confident that this will be the first in a long line of events we'll have at the farm, as you rise and rise in state government. It's important that we find someone who can handle events with us, for our future."

"You're planning ahead, I admire your organizational skills, Meredith, the best."

જી

"Miss Raymer, I love chemistry and your class. I'm not sure I've got my A sewed up for the third term. I'd like to do a special project to ensure the A. You are so knowledgeable, but I understand you can't have me do anything in your old field."

"Sit down, Mason, I appreciate you stopping by. A lab'll be starting in about five minutes. I do have something that might interest you. It'll involve leg work on your part, and seeking lab help, from water quality folks, maybe from our county water folks, got wheels?"

She watched him smile to her and nod his head. Her explanation seemed to suit him.

"I'll do it, Miss Raymer, a challenge, and maybe answer your question."

After the next AP class lecture, he stayed a minute to read through the project she wrote out for him.

"Can't wait to see what our little old microscopes have to say about what I bring in. Then I can compare those results with what the water quality folks come up with."

"It'll help me too, Mason, maybe answer a couple of questions that I couldn't answer 20 years ago, when I lived on my family's farm near Porttown. I guess my curiosity, it was what helped steer me to chemistry."

જી

On the way to see her OBGYN she sealed the decision in her mind. She and Colin discussed and agreed, nearly every time they were together after she discovered she was pregnant.

"Schedule the amniocentesis," Meredith requested of her doctor.

"What are good dates for you?"

"Colin and I will be married on Saturday, February 11. Wow, I can say it now, we've got a wedding date."

Dr. Farley watched the sparkle in Meredith's honey-colored eyes.

"I'm happy for you both, Meredith; you're seeming to be in a much better place than when you were here the first time."

"Yeah, I had frustration, worse, deep despair."

"How's he feeling about the baby."

"From the second I told him, he's ecstatic. And we've made a decision together."

"Decision?"

"As I said schedule the tests; it's a must. We'll figure out everything once we get the test results. I grew up as part of a family with special needs, uncle and brother, you know," Meredith nodded to the doctor.

"Abortion?"

"I hate to say it, but yes, if the fetus is in trouble. I know that a child is a gift from God, a gift. I also know what special needs does to a family. My mom finally walked away after all those years. She bore the brunt of the care for her son and her brother-in-law. It was her only way of coping. We lost her."

Meredith felt the tears streaming down her face as she shook her head. Her voice cracked, "I lost my mom. And I've never really grieved over that."

"In looking at the calendar I'll schedule tests at about the 15th week."

"You'll really have good evidence by that time, whether or not the fetus has abnormalities, right?"

Dr. Farley nodded to her.

Meredith paused, looking from her doctor to the calendar on the wall, "March, that sounds excellent, Dr. Farley. And if the fetus is OK, I'll want to take childbirth classes, but Colin won't be home until May."

"May will work."

℁

Meredith agreed to meet Mason at the farm one Saturday morning at 11. Together they walked to the water tank next to the windmill. She helped him break the thick layer of ice. She showed him how deep he would need to go to gather a water sample.

"Please do this three times, space the samples several days apart. I'll provide the samples from inside the farm home."

They each drove the mile to the water tank where Meredith wanted him to take the next sample.

"This is what's left of my old farm. We'll only have the one sample, and the water's been in the tank for a while. This is the only well and windmill on the farm."

"Miss Raymer, you're looking for pesticide in the water, aren't you?"

"Among other things, I am. Let's see what YOU find, Mason, remember this is your project. I first wanted to know about the water quality while I was at the university. But so much else happened, I never got around to checking."

"And I need to do the process three times, right?"

"Correct, space the samples a few days apart, and this is for the two different water locations."

"Then move on to the second step?"

She nodded to him, "You're on your way, Mason. I'll be anxious to learn what you discover."

"Me too," he smiled to her. "Uh, you'll get me the three different samples from your kitchen faucet?"

"Right, just let me know and I'll bring them to class the next day."

℃

"Meredith, you're stunning, where did you find this lovely dress?"

"At a bridal shop, it's a mother-of-the-bride dress, but perfect for lots of occasions, coming along for me."

"It will be, hem a little higher in the front than the back, high neckline, long sleeves, your beige shoes match the dress color exactly. Who did your greenery in your hair?"

"A wonderful young helper from the Flower Shop, who also created Christmas wreaths for my family's graves."

"Does reverend know of your situation?"

Meredith shook her head, "No one but you know. The amniocentesis is a ways off."

"That's right; you and Colin, after all this time, I'm so happy for you both. Let's go meet your groom."

Meredith and Jess hugged. They walked from a back room of the church down the aisle to meet Colin and Sam. Meredith held a single red rose with its greenery.

"Please go ahead with your words for each other," Reverend Forest said after they exchanged vows.

They held hands as they remembered their sayings.

Meredith began, "Be near me at the break of dawn, when dew kisses the flowers, I need your love just as the earth needs rain, as the sky needs the sun."

Colin replied, "Your smile, I need it as the bright noon sun caresses your hair, your cheeks," he spoke as he touched her cheek. "You'll walk down our rose-bordered stone walk, a picture of loveliness there."

He gave her his wide smile.

"I want to hear the sound of your voice, Colin, to be with you wherever you are."

Colin squeezed her hands in his, "God will gently close the curtain of night, and keep us safe together, watching the starlit skies above."

They kissed and began their life together.

℘

Guests danced in an area set aside for the DJ. He played many 80's and 90's songs. Colin twirled Meredith during their first dance as a married couple, to the requested song, *Annie.* They spent the rest of the afternoon mingling with company. As requested in the invitation, they wanted only the presence of the folks who joined them. Guests came and went, eating finger food and cake, wishing the couple a happy life. Meredith met over 150 people for the first time.

"The enormity of what he does," Meredith thought to herself as the afternoon waned, "and of the number of people that are affected, it's hard for me to fathom. I'm so glad Jess suggested a guest book, oh gosh, she just hosted everything, wow, Sam helped too."

Colin thanked the catering crew for their efforts as he paid them.

"You all are great, even remembering jumper cables for our guest who left his lights on out on the county highway."

The catering leader laughed, "We end up helping with all kinds of situations."

"Including sweeping up our floors," Colin said as he watched the rest of the catering crew nod their heads. A couple of the crew grinned to him about a catering memory.

The quiet caught them by surprise as they found Jess and Sam putting final touches to replacing the great room furniture where it belonged.

Meredith set cake and coffee down at the end table.

"You two go help yourselves. The crew kept what was left out for us to enjoy. The crowd ate every bit of the finger food. Join us, please," he indicated as he pointed to the couch.

Colin loosened his red tie after he sat down to his food. They returned with their cake and coffee.

He directed his gaze to them, "Thank you for everything, Jess and Sam, you truly made everyone feel at home."

They nodded to him.

"It's been an unforgettable day," Meredith touched Colin's shoulder, "joining our lives together."

He found her hand on his shoulder and enclosed his hand in hers.

&

Several weeks went by. Meredith drove to Des Moines to spend a Saturday night with Colin. On her way back Sunday afternoon she stopped by the Raymer farm. She trudged to the barn and looked around inside, a place of happy remembrances for her, chemistry experiments, working with her dad in his office, seeing Uncle Milt in his apartment in the back part of the barn, with Jeepers.

"Jeepers, oh Jeepers, sometimes I miss our dog a lot. I wonder if we could get a dog," she thought of the quiet at her Sanderson home. It would liven things up, especially if, if there's not a baby."

She closed the barn door and locked it. She leaned against the wood.

"Right now, I miss my family, mom wasn't at the wedding. I miss dad, Conner, Uncle Milt."

She got down on her knees in the snow and pressed her head against the side of the barn.

"Right now, I want to be with them, my family. I must be so hormonal, I don't feel really good, the baby's weighing on my mind, always in my thoughts. It's driving me nuts waiting more weeks just to have the tests done. I think it's gonna be bad news. Why wait so long to find out? I think I want to end the pregnancy now. Dr. Farley gave me the names of two doctors who will do the procedure. This mess is affecting everything I'm doing, at school, with Colin. We both have so much on our minds, so much in love, but our lives."

Meredith lifted her head from the wood and banged her right hand against the barn.

"What am I doing; I'm so screwed up right now," she screamed out.

Meredith planned what she needed to accomplish. It would be a long taxi ride for her but she felt she could tell no one about what she planned. Colin needed to stay in Des Moines for the weekend. At school she wrote out lesson plans if she needed to be out on Friday.

Her appointment was for 7 p.m. on Thursday. She felt sicker and sicker to her stomach as the taxi driver approached the town. For many nights now she woke in a sweat from nightmares she remembered, huge ghostie faces laughing, then crying, then singing eerie songs. After that she could not fall asleep, so she lay in bed and said prayers until time to get up for school. She paid cash for the procedure and waited in the room for the doctor to appear. His manner was brisk, but caring as he asked her a series of questions.

"We'll be in shortly; the medication will take hold; it won't take long."

She started to feel more relaxed as the nurse prepped her. Then she left Meredith alone.

Something flashed in front of her eyes. It was Colin's face, his young face from after his brother committed suicide. It was a face lined with pain, of sadness for his brother. After that her mind blasted her with bloody fetuses, Down Syndrome children and adults, white ghostly faces, shrieking and screaming in her head.

"It's the drugs, and it's God talking to me through the images and sounds. Meredith, what are you doing, are you out of your mind?"

She closed her eyes, as anger and sadness together seemed to seep into her pores. She counted to 100 and bolted upright from the operating table. She scooted to the edge and moved her legs out and down to the floor. With a careful movement she took the tape and IV from the vein on the top of her hand and held her finger over the tiny wound. As her head got clearer she dressed. After she flung her coat over her shoulders, Meredith walked out of the room. At the front desk, she simply shook her head and told the receptionist she would reschedule if the amniocentesis and other tests detected abnormalities. The receptionist nodded her head and called the same taxi driver to pick her up. Within 10 minutes she headed back to Porttown.

"I'm feeling a little tired; I'll rest now," she told the driver.

She closed her eyes. In her mind she observed Colin, the Colin he was now. He stood aways from her, a smile on his face, his arms held out, to welcome her. The trip home went quick for her. She handed the taxi driver the fare and a generous tip.

"Ma'am, you gonna be OK?" he asked.

She opened the door and got out in a slow fashion.

"Oh, thanks for asking, just sleepy, yeah I'm OK, would you mind waiting until I get inside."

"Glad to."

She gave him a tiny smile and waved. With small steps she made her way into their farm home, locked and dead bolted the door. She held on to the stair railing for dear life as she took the steps to the second floor in a slow motion. She dropped her purse and coat on the floor and crawled into bed.

℘

Meredith perched on a stool in the lab. She finished with her two classes and finalized her lesson plans for the next week's lectures and lab.

The pound pounding in her head began to dissipate.

"That's the stupid medication I got last night; that stuff and I just don't get along. I'm really allergic, I am."

She put her head down on the lab counter and listened to the quiet beating of her heart. Meredith put her hand on her stomach. It still felt rock hard, as it always had since her early days.

"Baby child, I almost lost you. And for God's sake, Colin didn't know what I was doing. I wonder if I'll ever get the nerve to tell him, what almost happened. God, thank you for whatever it was You did last night. I didn't save our baby," she spoke out. "But You did," she whispered.

She raised her head, her eyes stained with tears.

"Today is a precious day, with my precious baby still with me."

℘

On her way home that Friday Meredith finally remembered. She shut her cell phone off the evening before as she waited in the room to have the abortion. And she completely spaced out turning it back on. She listened to four messages from Colin. The first three asked her to call him back. His voice sounded panicked in the fourth one.

"Meredith, I'm super concerned. I won't be able to get home this weekend; it's very late, where are you? Dear one, are you OK?"

By then Meredith noted a tone of panic in Colin's voice.

She shook her head as she thought, "I was so out of it, by the time I got home, from relief, from the drugs, I couldn't a talked to you if I'd wanted to. I was so dead out; I passed out with all my clothes on. Dear God, what'll I tell Colin?"

She left him a message about being tired yesterday, that she turned her cell off after arriving home and didn't get it turned back on until she just listened to his messages.

"That's my story, at least until I learn the truth about our baby," she whispered.

That night Meredith flung herself, back and forth across the bed, after being so wigged out on premedication the evening before. About 2 a.m. she said prayers for the hundredth time and eased into a quiet sleep. In a dream she danced in a whirling dress barefooted around the Sanderson backyard. She held a baby in her arms.

The next morning she woke early following the sun as it rose in the eastern sky, watching from the French doors out to the patio.

"Saturday morning, and Colin won't be home. What do I want to do with this precious time?"

She sat, having her second cup of coffee at the kitchen island. Then she got busy. Boxes from her move out of the apartment and three small pieces of her furniture stacked up in the back of the garage. She separated everything, dividing up what would go to donation and the few things she wanted in her new home. Her cell rang.

"Meredith, it's mom."

"Mom, I, uh, everything OK?"

"Yes it is. Your welcome reception invitation, it was so lovely, with the red rose on the cover. At the last minute I ended up not being able to come for your wedding day and festivities.   My helpers told me they could handle everything. It was Valentine's week. Then one of them got sick, so I ended up working almost through one night, to get caught up on our Valentine's orders. I never called you to explain."

"Yeah, I remember that busy week, from working in the shop here in town."

"You took over for me."

"I did, all those years ago."

I, I'm calling to ask you to consider taking me back into your life."

"Just like that?"

"You know I've never had much to say, so just like that."

"What do you propose, Mom?" she asked as politely as she could. Meredith felt her face flame up, scalding tears hurting her eyes.

"After Easter, and before Mother's Day and graduations, we get kinda a break in the action at my flower shop. I would like to visit you and Colin. I understand you're with your students. And I don't know where he is in his legislative session. It would just be for a Saturday and Sunday. I'd rent a car and drive from the Des Moines airport."

Meredith wiped her eyes and nose and took a deep breath, "I need to think about it. And I'll check with Colin to see what he's got going on. Give me your possible dates and I'll get back to you."

"Thank you, Meredith. Please let me know."

"You want to donate all of these nice things to the Thrift Shop?"

"I just went through stuff from the past 20 years of my life. It's time to let go of this," she nodded to the volunteer who helped her take items from the back of her SUV.

Meredith felt good about giving up some of the little silly things she picked up during her trips with the Air Force.

"My life is way different now, and I have a few little reminders left, that's enough. This is just a tiny way for me to give back."

Her cell rang; she checked the ID.

"Hey Meredith, surprise, I got away, just for this Saturday night, hafta head back tomorrow. I'm excited to see you. Uh, when you get home we gotta talk. I got the mail from our mailbox and just went through it. There's a bill from a doctor, not your Dr. Farley, not in Porttown. Help me here."

In as light a voice as she could muster Meredith answered, "Can explain soon as I get home. Should be there in 10 minutes."

She prayed 15 of *The Lord's Prayer* in a very slow voice. She said, "I am blessed; I am grateful" a number of times. With her straight posture and eyes gazing straight ahead, she approached Colin in their kitchen. They kissed and hugged.

"Criminy, shit," she thought to herself.

She stepped back from him and waited for his question.

"I, uh, help me, $35 for medication, an office visit, on Thursday, in Billingham?"

He held on to the bill.

"That's correct, I was there."

Tell him, her mind screamed as she thought about how fast that bill came.

"I was at an abortion clinic; I got it in my mind that I couldn't wait for the amniocentesis. I was so sure of an abnormal fetus. But I didn't have the abortion. I'm still carrying our baby."

"For the love of heaven, why didn't you tell me what you were planning? Unbelievable, you wanted to abort before you knew? Oh Meredith, that baby is mine, too. Oh man, I'm super upset. What if you'd gone through with it? When had you planned on telling me? You've always been honest with me."

She watched his tears come as he kept shaking his head at her.

"I can only tell you this; I was totally screwed up in my head. And I did not realize what was happening until I got the IV. Then it hit me that this was not what God wanted for me, for us. I realized I have to wait for the test results."

"Meredith, you must come to me, talk to me, when this kind of thing hits you. I know you lived with mental retardation in your brother and uncle until you went to college. And I can only imagine what all those years must have done to your mom."

"Yeah, she walked away, done and done," Meredith slammed her hand down on the counter as she burst into tears.

They moved to each other and hugged. Colin stepped back from Meredith.

"I'm sleeping in the guest bedroom tonight, Meredith. I gotta think about everything that's just happened. And I gotta get back tomorrow morning. Maybe if you go to church and talk to God, it'll help you. I plan to pray a lot tonight, don't know if I'll be able to sleep."

He moved his overnight bag into a guest bedroom from their room.

"I'll fix something for myself, maybe toasted cheese, for dinner. I'm going for a walk now. I know you got school work and horn practice. You go ahead with that stuff. I just don't want to talk; I need to think, Meredith."

"Me too, faith and trust, those are issues that I gotta work out."

That night they both cried a lot, in their separate beds. In the morning Colin heard Meredith down in the kitchen, making coffee and listening to the radio. He showered and got everything put back in his bag.

"Good morning."

She heard the sad tone of his voice as he avoided giving her eye contact. He folded his arms across his chest.

"Good morning, I heard some winter birds chirping out back. Colin, before you leave I need to let you know my mom called. She wants to visit us, in April, after Easter, before graduation and all the stuff that comes after that in a flower shop."

Colin grinned to her, "Oh Meredith, yes, please ask her. Wow, I remember what a slim and pretty woman she was. I think it would be wonderful if you two could reconcile. It's been a long long time."

"OK, I'll take care of it, stay for breakfast?"

"Nah, I gotta get back; I had a chance to think last night, didn't sleep much."

"I didn't either."

He stood across from her and downed a half cup of coffee. He came to her and they hugged.

"Safe travels."

They gazed into each other's eyes as they stepped away from each other.

Colin gave her an unsmiling nod and walked out of their home.

&

Meredith talked to God that Sunday morning, more than she had in a very long time. That talk continued after she attended church and shook hands with Reverend Forest after the service. Two couples stopped and chatted. They now recognized her as Colin's wife, from the wedding reception the couples attended.

"How's Colin?"

"In the thick of the legislative session; issues keep them so busy. He really enjoys everything he does at the capitol."

"Glad to hear it."

They walked away from each other, with smiles on both sides and good lucks for the remaining session. Meredith almost stopped at Jess's home, deciding that she just could not reveal this latest issue, her almost abortion. She and God kept talking.

&

Two weeks went by. Meredith received one e-mail from Colin. He made no indication as to when he might come home for a weekend. He just mentioned being crazy busy, which Meredith understood. In an e-mail back to him she told him the time and date of the amniocentesis and other tests.

She called her mom.

"Hey, that weekend will work fine with me. What about Colin?"

"Never know, he wants to see you; we'll see how his workload and the sessions are panning out."

Meredith and her mom planned out the details. Meredith and Jess got together at Jess's for coffee. They hugged. She shared with her about her mom. Meredith watched the smile on Jess's face.

"This is a good thing, Meredith, her wanting to reconcile with you, especially good, the timing, you know, she's coming after the amniocentesis. No matter the results, it'll be good for you to be in contact with your mom. You'll have decisions to make, either way the tests go."

"That's right; mom'll get to see me play my corn planting role. When she comes is about time to plant corn. I'm taking a couple days off to help with the effort. We have to plant my stuff and Colin's too."

"Ooowww, he'll be near the end of his legislative session."

"Uh huh, he won't get home. His part-timer will run the show as he has for the past few years. Babe and me, we'll just try to stay out of the way," Meredith laughed.

4

"Precious babe, inside me, thank you God, babe, you're a normal fetus, I am very grateful," Meredith breathed out.

Relief brought just the opposite effect for her. She watched her shaking hands and felt hot tears roll down her cheeks. She phoned Colin and caught him getting ready for bed in Des Moines.

"Oh, Meredith, oh thanks God," he paused and his voice started to choke, "for your blessings bestowed upon us; did you ask about the baby's gender?"

"No, don't wanna know, as long as babe is healthy, which we know is the case so far, early day tomorrow?"

"Jammed, I'm so excited for us. The doc says you're doing OK?"

"Yeah, not gaining much weight, gonna be one of those gals who gains just a little bit, and carries babe way inside. I'm not even gonna show, until about seventh or eighth month. That's good 'cause of our heat and humidity, I'll handle that much better."

"That's just grand news."

"You've got your political agenda when the session ends, being all over your district, and setting up your campaign office, right?"

"Uh huh, it'll be an exciting time, baby in August, the election in November."

"I took our income tax information to our accountant. It's best to keep everything separated, your land, crop, assets, and my land, crop, military pension."

"Just like we been doing it, the last few years, since we lost your dad. Meredith, I'm still not ready to come home for a weekend. I'll try really hard to come for a partial day, maybe a Saturday afternoon, when your mom comes."

"That'll be good, Colin, I appreciate that for mom."

When they hung up, Meredith made up a pot of coffee and sat drinking it, her second cup.

"It may be awhile, maybe into May, before he decides he's ready to come home. I know he's still very angry with me. Time, it'll take time, would'a been terrible if I'd gone through with it. I'd a never known what could be, this child we will have. I think this'll haunt me, my actions, 'til the day I die."

Meredith nodded at her thought and put her head on her hands on the kitchen countertop and bawled. She cried for a long time. After she calmed down, she started praying out loud, prayer after prayer.

ℴℴ

"Mrs. Sanderson, uh I gotta remember to call you that, I'm really happy with the A on my project and the A for third quarter. What do you think of the test results?"

"Very pleased, Mason, with your detailed organization of the water samples, the results of your interview with the water district official, and your conclusion, based on the hypothesis you proposed."

"Thank you, I'm glad you asked me to stop by after class. I saw the project grade, but I still wanted to talk to you."

"The one thing the project certainly showed me was the diminished lead content in the water coming into our farm home."

"Uh huh, based on the high lead content from the water at the Raymer farm."

"The difference, I believe, Mason, was that Colin replaced every single bit of pipe as he had his home reconstructed."

"So the old pipe, lead, possibly caused problems in the old days."

"Right, that's the pipe that brought in the water Colin's parents, and Colin and his brother drank. And his folks died way young, before their time."

"Connection?"

Mason watched Meredith nod her head, "Years back Colin and I wondered for sure, about that, the pesticides and lead."

ℂ

"Mom, join me in the kitchen, would you like coffee?"

"Of course, drink it by the gallons at work."

"What do you think of what Colin's done?"

"Your home is just right, for you two, for a family one day. You remember our small little farm houses, from your growing up days. Corn helped make this area prosperous. I noticed several other farms on the way here, their homes updated."

"Did you know our farm house burned down?"

She watched her mom's lips tighten as she shook her head.

"I did not; I'm sorry, renters after your dad died?"

"There were."

They finished their coffee and sugar cookies.

"Let me show you out back; Ted and his helper are beginning to get the planting done, both on Sanderson and Raymer fields. I just helped out with seed selection and pesticide; they're doing the rest. The fields finally dried out enough. High quality seeds're going into the ground. The technology is excellent now, for the kind of seed that a corn grower needs, based on his particular pest problem in his particular area. Now days they call it integrated pest management Also the fertilizers, the chemistry in them, is way better than it was back in the day. Mostly it's the nitrogen levels, we have a better handle on them than in the past."

"With your chem background, you can certainly determine the good or bad fertilizers and what they can do to the ground, to the water table, the aquifer."

"Uh huh, that's been an interesting aspect of the planting and care of the corn, a lot of it's chemistry-based, I love that."

They walked along the edge of a field within a few hundred yards of the back yard.

"Come closer, you see this green, coming up. It's a change from your time. This is alfalfa living mulch, somethin' I didn't know anything about, but Colin and Ted, they been planting this way for some years."

"Alfalfa, in a corn field," Julie shook her head to Meredith, "don't understand."

"Got it, neither did I; it's called a vegetative buffer zone, 20 feet or so wide. What happens now is the vegetation is planted, then the corn is planted on either side of the vegetation. Corn stays moister, and the soil erosion is lessened. Oh, and another thing, corn alternates with soy beans. Uh huh," she stopped and looked out across the field, "we alternate one year a field is soy beans, next year it's corn. They do that on 2/3 thirds of all the fields, the last 1/3 stays planted in corn all the time."

Julie smiled to her daughter, "Scientific, my goodness."

"Yes Mom, all farmers gotta be part scientist now. We're contending with soil erosion and groundwater pollution."

"What's your plan after planting?"

"Right, our home'll go back to quiet, from the noise in the fields. I got a couple of ideas of what I want to do."

Julie turned to her daughter and smiled, "Tell me."

"I'd like to get a Jeepers."

Julie paused, her mind scrolling back to the dog that was her only company at times in the Raymer farm house, for the few hours the kids were in school and she wasn't working.

"One fabulous, loving dog," she nodded.

"And our Porttown Symphony, I'm a French horn player in it, we'll have our spring concert a couple of weeks before school's out, oh and of course I have my students for a few more weeks."

"Glad you kept the horn up; it's got such a caressing sound."

Meredith heard the complimentary tone of her mom's voice.

They strode with long steps back to the home.

"I forgot how beautiful you are, Mom," Meredith said.

"And I never saw a picture of you after your 16th birthday; you are beautiful, Meredith, tall, strong, straight, a real military officer. You have a bearing that'll never leave you."

Meredith nodded to her mom, "And wait 'til you see Colin. He's more handsome, as time goes on. There's a beginning of a ruggedness, I guess from farm life, that's replaced his young-looking face."

Julie paused as she looked down, "Oh Meredith, a rose garden, it must be beautiful, do you remember our rose garden in the back?"

"I do, Conner and I named one of the roses after you, it helped us, a living representation of you."

"That was special, what you did for Conner, thanks."

Meredith choked down the mucous beginning to drain down her throat. She felt no tears come to her eyes. She stooped down and pointed at a bush Colin explained to her.

"This one's a red rose bush, and Colin's got a bright yellow bush, this one, to remember his mom by," she turned to her mom. "The rest I'll discover about this summer. Colin said he'd be in charge of the whole back yard, including the rose garden. He's gonna teach me a little about rose gardening."

"Good, there's kinda a trick to it."

Colin arrived and joined them in the kitchen. He hugged his mother-in-law.

"May I call you Julie?"

Julie smiled to him, "Please."

"Your flight and travels here?"

"Fine."

"We'll have dinner early, and maybe play a game after that. My memory tells me you were a bunch of game players at the Raymer house."

"We were," Julie and Meredith spoke in unison, looked at each other and laughed.

℣

"The meal's delicious, ham flavor so nice and smoked, and scalloped potatoes, uuummm."

"Not mine, the potatoes, Mom, good old Betty Crocker, she does so much tasty stuff for me. I never did much cooking for all my military years, so I'm just getting back into the swing of cooking as I did back in the day."

Meredith nodded her head to Colin.

"Julie, we have news for you. In late August you'll be a grandma."

Julie blinked to them, then blinked again. They watched her eyes light up.

She put her hand to her throat, then patted her heart. She held Colin's hand and Julie's hand.

"God bless and keep this family, and this babe."

Then she smiled to them. She started to speak.

"Uh, Mom, I know what you're gonna ask; yes, all the necessary tests," she nodded her head, "accomplished, fetus is AOK; and no, we did not ask about the babe's gender. We'll love him or her."

"Healthy," Colin interjected.

"I wish to God those tests were more available when you kids were all born."

Julie shook her head, the memory of Conner and Milt smacking her mind. She dropped her eyes, looking at her plate. Meredith saw a sadness, a pursing of her mom's lips.

"Uh, would you like to visit Conner's, dad's and Uncle Milt's graves?"

Julie remained silent. Meredith watched her mom raise her eyes to her. Tears glittered in them and squashed out the corners of her eyes.

Julie nodded.

Colin consented to join them on their trip to the Porttown cemetery.

"I haven't been to the graves of dad and mom, Cole, and my grandparents for many years. This'll be an early Memorial Day visit from us all."

Meredith took them to the Raymer family area. She and Colin went to another part of the cemetery, the burial area of his family.

"I wanted mom to have some time alone there. And wow, I do not even remember this area, well it's 20 some plus years since I was here standing behind you at Cole's memorial."

"You took wreaths to your family's graves at Christmas, right?"

"I did."

"I'd like to make that a family tradition for us, as our babe grows. Our babe has only one grandparent, Julie. It'll be important that our baby knows where he or she came from."

"That's right, Colin, we're a mighty small family."

They held hands as they walked back to the area where Julie stood. They watched as she stepped forward and put her hand on top of Conner's grave.

Then she turned to Meredith and Colin.

"Unbelievable, I did not even come back for my own son's funeral. I was one messed up person; I'm better now. Thank you so much for bringing me out here, somethin' I needed to do for a long time."

Colin looked at Julie, thinking, "That's the most words I've ever heard her speak. Maybe she's coming out of her shell as pretty much of a mute. I know she's gotta be more personable at her flower shop."

"We're glad to do it, Mom. It helps us too."

On the drive back to their home, Julie spoke up, "Meredith explained about the corn and the soybeans. Wow, planting, production, the whole situation's changed since ethanol's come into the mix."

"For sure, Julie, I've been part of the state and national corngrower's groups for many years now. It's interesting, and exciting, and it sure's been a part of what I do with the state legislature. I work alongside lawyers, agriculture service folks, and every other kind of individual you can imagine."

He gave them a laugh as he said that, 'Nuf of me, tell us about your flower shop."

"Peaks and valleys, rush and quiet times in the shop, also a wedding planner, learned that when I still lived in Porttown. We do a number of weddings each year plus flowers and other arrangements, love it all."

"Yeah, Mom, we took over for you, Dena and I did, after you moved to Santa Barbara. You'd planned quite a few weddings that summer I was home."

"Fun?"

"Certainly were, you had a notebook with lots of information on each one of the weddings. We had a good time, attended every single reception. And I had one bride who was super grateful to me right before her wedding."

"What'd you do?"

"Well, you were prepared for every emergency. In the packet we took to each wedding, there was a small sewing kit, needles, little scissor, and several different colors of thread, white, ivory, beige. A bride ripped out four inches of material under the right arm of her dress. I patched her up within 10 minutes."

Julie raised up from the back seat and patted Meredith's shoulder as she sat up front on the passenger side.

"Meredith, I really tried to prepare you for any possibility, at home and also at the shop."

She turned back to her mom.

"You really did," she smiled to Julie.

ℤ

They stood face to face in their bedroom. She took his hand in hers.

"So sorry, Colin, no excuse, I messed up. I gotta learn to share, trust, that's such a critical part of our relationship. Is there any way I can help, help you get through this?"

He shook his head.

"I'm sorry it's taken me so long to figure out this. For a while I lost faith in you, Meredith. But I'm getting that faith back. You're doing everything, as you always have and will, helping with the planting, teaching, playing in the symphony. You're busy. I haven't been happy, but I'm getting that back too. I forgive you."

He watched her tears, coming hard.

"I'm happy now, with the test results, sad that I've caused you such mind-blowing agony. And my mom, I've sorta forgotten all the sadness and anger she evoked in me for so long after she left us. Really, I just loved dad, and I had to let her go. But that's changed, I put myself in mom's shoes, with her situation, especially when I realized that I might bear an abnormal fetus. I now can understand pretty much her despair, having a Down Syndrome baby, Conner, still loving and caring for him as she did."

"Conner did great; he became a fine man, I saw that, Meredith, while you were gone all those years in the military. Your mom had everything to do with his days through high school."

"Agree."

He cupped her chin and began to raise it to his lips, "But you, you inspired your brother, your fine example and being close to him and loving him. He loved you so, so much. Dear one, you've a huge capacity for caring; I see it, your students see it."

He gave her a soft gentle kiss, then pressing his lips on her cheeks and the side of her throat. They nestled in each other's arms after becoming one in gentle lovemaking.

After, they moved to their sides, facing each other, "I've missed you terribly."

"I've missed you more," Colin whispered back.

They laughed to each other, as they drifted off to sleep.

∞

They saw Julie off early the next morning. She promised she would come back to visit her grandbaby. And, as Colin agreed, he and Meredith removed the double bed from the bedroom down the hall from theirs.

"You're so tough, Meredith, like that whole task didn't bother you a bit."

"Strength training, it'll always be a part of my pt."

They set the bed up as a day bed in one corner of the large finished-off room in the basement.

"I have to head out; when is Amanda Cowden bringing by the baby bed?

"Over the weekend, I ordered the new mattress for the bed. It'll be delivered next Thursday. Hey, she's bringing it all set up in the back of their pickup. We don't have to learn how to put together a baby bed."

"Awesome."

"That's what Amanda mentioned; she and Adam had quite a time with the instructions for the bed, didn't quite match what really needed to be done."

"You're positive they want to give the bed up?"

"Uh huh, she said they're done, 5 and 3, both boys, they gave up any idea of getting a girl."

"Changing table?"

"A faculty member at school is donating theirs to us; I saw it. It'll work just fine. And Stewart's only request was that when we're done with the table we pass it along to someone else with a baby coming. I put money down and have a hold on a sweet rocking chair at the Thrift Shop. We'll be set with all that."

They walked up to their bedroom, hand in hand.

"It shouldn't be too much longer; we might run over again this legislative session. I hope to be home for the

Senior Prom, and for your Spring Fling of the Porttown Symphony."

"I hope so too," Meredith touched his cheek.

℃

"Need your help, Meredith," Dawn Deevers smiled to her as they stood together in her classroom after her class left.

"What's up?"

"I'm the vice-principal charged with working all non-athletic school activities. Our faculty member helping to sponsor the Porttown Senior Prom is out for the rest of the year, family-related issue. A sub is covering her classes, but I need a faculty member to ride herd on the planning and execution of the prom. Here's the e-mail from her regarding her work with the prom committee."

Meredith read through the information and nodded her head to Dawn, "The students pretty much got this handled. The Jennifer on this committee is one of my AP chem students. I'll help."

Meredith thought, "Fun, it'll be fun, I never had a senior prom, too anxious to get on to college."

The next day she asked Jennifer to remain after chem lab for a minute.

"Oh Mrs. Sanderson, thank you; Mrs. Deevers saw me this morning and told me you would help us out. Our committee's awesome: we'll get 'er done."

Meredith watched the shine in Jennifer's eyes. They agreed on a date and time when Meredith could meet with the committee. The students carried on the meeting in the cafeteria after school. They asked for Meredith's input.

"I feel you've got everything under control; having it in the grand ballroom in the Porttown Hotel sounds very nice. And I'm glad the hotel's only allowing you to do just a bit of decorating. I looked over your budget; the savings on decorations, well, that's a smart move so you can pay more for this good DJ you rave about. The dancing is the super big deal of this event, right?"

Meredith watched the smiles and nods from the committee members.

"Mrs. Sanderson, we'll just need you to check on the decorations Saturday afternoon. If your husband can come, we'll have an extra chaperone."

"So hoping he'll be able to get here from Des Moines; we have two sets of parents helping?"

"Correct."

"I approve of the catering crew; it's the same group Colin and I used for our reception in February."

"That was the day your name changed, right?"

"It was; we had so much fun, and the caterers, excellent."

"Somebody'll be standing by the punch bowl, that's for sure."

"I assure you, folks, the caterers will handle the punch bowl. What happens to everyone after the dance is out of this committee's control," Meredith commented.

"Hey, guys, guys, Mrs. Sanderson may not know this, but," Jennifer nodded to Meredith, "there's an after-prom at the auxiliary gym at school. I imagine most kids will go from the prom to the after-prom."

"Wow, that's a nice gesture, a bunch of parents doing that for you all?" Meredith asked as her eyes went around for confirmation.

The group nodded, "They are," almost in unison.

"We'd like you and your husband to join us at after-prom, if you want to."

"I'll check in with him, OK?" Meredith nodded to the group.

ℴℴ

"Hey, I can't get home; stuff's jammin' up here, so much to do before end of session."

"Yeah Colin," she paused, "it's OK, I just have to check on everything prior to the dance, you know, with the decorations, table setups, and the caterer's area. The class is using the caterer we used for our wedding reception."

"Everything'll be OK; you'll just have to stay for the dance, and can leave, right?"

"Uh huh, I'm skipping the after-prom, that's a kid and parent deal."

"I love you, have a good time, wearing your stunner dress from our wedding?"

"I am, and my wonderful bracelet."

"Great dress, I love you, hope to be home for the Spring Fest with the symphony."

"If you can, I know you're getting close, but the decisions you make, they'll impact all of us."

"Gosh, for the better, for all Iowa folks."

"I love you, big push, good luck, Colin."

℘

To Meredith's surprise Sam brought Jess to the prom. She watched them walk in and shake hands with parent chaperones. They circulated, working the room, chatting with students, and stopping to talk to the caterers. They got their punch and asked a young couple if they could join them at their table. Meredith decided that's what all folks in supervisory positions did. She remembered the few formal ceremonies that required her presence back in her military days.

"Nah, I don't miss those times at all," she thought as she moved around the room, chatting with the few students, her chemistry students, that she knew.

Mostly she stood back, enjoying the young people, their high spirits, and their abundant supply of energy.

"May I have this dance?"

"Mason, hello, how are you?"

He smiled to her as they waltzed to a song Meredith hummed, from before his time.

"I'm good, liking the DJ, uh, what's the song, Mrs. Sanderson, that you're humming?"

"It's called *Moon River*, a waltz from the 1960's."

"Sweet."

He led her back to where she stood before.

"Thank you, Mason; it was fun," she gave him her wide smile.

Most of the girls and some of the guys joined in the line dance which the DJ played next. Meredith got in the back of the line, beginning to remember the steps she learned dancing with Colin when she came back to Porttown after retiring. Her mind whirled through the important events of her life these past few months: loving Colin, her students, teaching them, the wedding and reception. She felt sharp pain stab her chest at the awful recollection of what almost happened to the fetus.

"Let it go, Meredith, it'll make you sick, let it go," the tape played over and over in her mind.

"May I have this dance?"

She turned, taking in a deep breath to smother her surprise.

"Yes, Sam, you like the fast ones?"

"I do."

He took her hand. And Meredith held on to his hand, as he twirled and twirled her in a fast swing dance. She watched his smile to her and smiled back.

"Thank you, Meredith, I haven't danced fast like that for years. I'll get Jess out on the floor in a little bit."

Meredith heard applause and looked around to see young couples standing around Sam and her.

"Mrs. Sanderson and Mr. Salton, oh you can dance, you can dance."

Meredith and Sam did what came natural, they smiled to each other again, and then bowed to the students.

Meredith heard the clapping get louder as whistles added to the applause.

Sam headed back to the table with Jess, and Meredith moved to the back area where she stood earlier.

"That was so fun," she mentioned to the students who stood near her.

"It was great," they complimented her.

She smiled and nodded to them and headed to the punch and cookies table.

ℬ

Colin sat next to Jess at the symphony's Spring Fest.

"She's worked hard, learning the French horn part. She admitted to me that some of the music was a real stretch for her abilities."

"Is Meredith keeping it up?"

"I think so, for now she's filling in for a player who had a baby. So maybe later, our little one will take some of her time. But she's wanted to perform for so many years and not really an opportunity while she was an officer, so a dream she's fulfilling."

"Right, especially in her field, the lab setting."

Colin searched through the program

"Aha, Copland's *Appalachian Spring*, the concluding piece of the concert, it's a great piece," Colin thought.

He saw other works, Mendelssohn's *Spring Song* and one he absolutely recognized, *Greensleeves*. From where they sat neither Jess nor Colin could see Meredith. Colin cocked his ear and from time to time in each piece he could hear the sweet pure tones of her horn playing.

"Masterful," Colin turned to Jess after the concert concluded.

"We have enormous talent, super brain power, in our community. I'm really proud of where I live, with lots of caring and concerned folks, like you and Meredith."

ℬ

"Want to go look at the field near the equipment shed, see what you think?"

"That sounds good, Meredith, then I gotta head out. Ted's e-mailed me about the planting progress. He appreciates your interest in everything that goes on. I know, I know, it's your corn on your land, it's just that there's never been a female interest in all this."

Meredith laughed, "Yeah, he'll get used to me, as years go by."

They walked, hand in hand, to the same field Meredith showed her mom while Julie visited.

"Everything looks great, Meredith, so far, providing the weather and the moisture cooperate."

"It's a long haul to October and harvesting the corn crop, Colin. I honestly don't remember that part, seemed to me that the corn came up, got ripe and got harvested."

"Yeah, that's a young person's view of how it happens."

She nodded to him, "Now I'm gonna see the real deal."

"You are," he picked her up and swung her around, "been wanting to do that for so long."

He set her down on her feet in a graceful motion.

"So, when school's out, dear one, get the dog that you want so much."

She kissed him on the lips, once, twice, three times.

"Jeepers."

"That's right, and one more thing, let me show you."

They walked the distance from the field to a fenced in pasture behind the Sanderson barn structure.

"You been talkin' about animals, on our farm. I don't have any right now, but I think I know what you might want to do."

He led her into the pasture through a solid closed gate.

"I've just kept this in grassland for the past few years. Before that I had a cow-calf setup. But I didn't have time to keep it up so I sold out. This is about one and a half acres. He pointed out the trees on the far end of the pasture.

"That's the water tank, that is, the water from the tank, that I used for the experiment I had one of my students do during the third quarter."

"Yeah, I remember, he was concerned about his grade."

"Uh huh, that young man will go on to do some great things after college. He's got an inquisitive mind, with lots of energy to devote to whatever cause he's into."

"Maybe, sometime, if you want to, you could do a cow-calf operation."

Meredith squeezed Colin's hand as they walked along.

"Yeah, that would be an interesting experience for me; getting a calf raised for sale as a young beef product, what a study in feeding habits."

"Another foray into chemistry, my dear, you will never leave your chosen field, there's so much chemistry in everything we do on this farm."

ᐫ

Meredith checked the school calendar hanging in the chem lab.

"I'm just barely going to manage gettting my AP kids through their final chapters and labs, just took time preparing them for their AP exam, my bad," she shook her head as she talked.

"I think most of them will do well on the exam, so that's my good," she nodded and smiled.

Meredith joined Jess for dinner at their favorite restaurant, to celebrate their final push to the end of the school year.

"Summer plans?"

"I still can't believe I'm having a baby in August, so I guess, finalizing the baby's room, watching the corn grow. Colin says to get a dog, so I'm going to look for Jeepers, want a not too big, friendly and devoted type, who'll be good around little children. I need to do what I can to help him with his reelection."

"Wow, this'll be for his third term."

"Yup," Meredith replied

"Hey, our women's guild at church, we're toying with the idea of adopting one of the elementary schools."

Jess saw Meredith's eyes light up, "Like, in watching over the students, making sure they have clothes, boots, for winter, enough food?"

"Oh yeah."

"Know which school?"

"Uh huh, the district's running summer school there."

"Oh my gosh, those little kids, Jess, I delivered Christmas boxes to at least one of those little ones."

"They are in our church."

"They have so very little."

Meredith stopped talking, thinking back at the shock she got while delivering the boxes, the abject poverty in her own community.

"So tell me."

"There's a great need for meals for these kids during the summer. You know we feed kids breakfast and lunch during the school year. So Food Bank is coordinating with the cafeteria at this particular school to have a Kid's Café this summer. And our guild members will volunteer with Food Bank volunteers to have the Café open on Monday, Wednesday, and Friday. At least three days a week needy kids can get a lunch meal that day."

"Believe there are kids from other schools who need help."

"Oh my gosh, that's so true, as long as somebody can get them to the school, Food Bank will feed them."

"Jess, I still can't believe it, during these starting-to-be-better times, we still have so many struggling families. I contribute to Food Bank."

"The answer is to continue to educate these young people, so they have better when they get older than their parents have had."

"Education is the answer," Meredith nodded to her.

Their food arrived.

"Oh I'm starved," Meredith whispered to Jess, "I'll eat hearty, but I gotta continue to count my own blessings, and to pray for all of us, kids, teachers, all of us."

—

Meredith fixed lasagna, garlic bread and salad for dinner. She and Colin spent time bringing in some of his possessions from the legislative session that he didn't want to leave at the apartment. Then they sat down and ate, enjoying each other's company as they had not been able to for many months.

"School's almost out; will you miss your students?"

"I will, but I'm gonna help out younger kids this summer."

"How's that?"

"Our church women's guild is volunteering at the Kid's Café this summer, from early June through the first week in August."

She went on to explain the impoverished young people in their own community and how they needed to have one decent meal three days a week at noon.

"I know you've other issues on your mind. I'm gonna help tend to our little people here."

Colin took her hand and kissed it as they finished their meal.

"My wife, helping while she can, before babe arrives. Are you enjoying the childbirth classes we're taking together?"

"They're OK; I'm just anxious to have our little one arrive."

"Room's all set?"

"Yup, and Amanda's given me all her kids' baby clothes, from birth on. I won't need to buy anything for some time, 'cause she's given me mostly stuff that's OK for a boy or a girl."

"You two becoming friends?"

"Hope too, not a lot of time yet, this summer, I'll spend time with her and her little ones."

"Meredith, let's take our cheesecake out on the patio with our coffee. There's somethin' we need to discuss."

"OK, got it."

They sat next to each other, looking out over the field of corn growing in the distance."

"Dear one?"

"Yes?" she turned to him, catching his blue eyes, pools of blue that she could almost drown in.

"You don't talk about him, but I know he's still in your heart, and in your memory. Sometimes you go to your Tyler place, that's what I call it."

She nodded to him as tears filled her eyes.

"Meredith, I want us to name our son, if we have a son, name him Tyler, and I would like to call him Ty. What about Tyler Jack?"

"Oh Colin," she felt her throat constrict, a lump of grief starting to choke her.

She coughed and coughed, her tears increasing.

"I still miss him, forever in my heart," she thought as she held her head in her hands.

Colin got her tissues, and she mopped her face and nose.

"Sorry, I haven't had a meltdown of grief like this for a long time. I, I," she stopped talking for several minutes. Meredith turned to him and touched his cheek with her fingers.

"Perfect," she said as he watched her nod to him. "Thank you for that thought. He'll have a great name."

"You already think it's a boy, don't you?"

"I do, never been around girls that much, especially in my Air Force work. I'm really enjoying some of the girls in my chem classes. There're very into their phones, their looks, boys, and messaging, but they have dreams, like I did, and still do have. I've talked to my classes about their hopes and dreams, most have already shared."

"Goin' on to school?"

Meredith nodded to Colin, "Planning to, one little piece of advice I give, if they're not sure, start small, get their basics at a community college. It'll help them figure out what they want to do at the big boy schools."

"Do you mention the savings of starting at the cc?"

"I do, but they tell me their counselors already talked to them about that."

"Good that the counselors do that," Colin gazed at her.

"Did I ever tell you that after dad and Conner died I socked a small part of their insurance money into a Roth IRA I continued to fund from 2005 until I retired in 2011?"

"Nope, there's still much we gotta get to know about each other's finances, but that's a smart move."

"Uh huh, that Roth, I now know, it's our babe's college fund, that's just 18 years from now."

"Unbelievable, that's not that much time, from birth to the university."

"At our age, we can see how quick that happens."

∞

Meredith helped little children, refilling their water glasses. Today the milk supply did not get delivered to Kid's Café.

"I haven't had any milk since I ate here on Friday," she heard that from a number of students who came to lunch that Monday.

Meredith explained to each child who mentioned that, "There was a breakdown in communication with our milk supplier. We'll try really hard to have milk for you on Wednesday."

"Thank you, ma'am," was the standard reply from the little ones.

When Meredith got home that afternoon she looked at her budget and decided she could give a little more each month to the Food Bank. She wrote out her check for mailing. She took her cup of iced coffee outside to the humid back porch.

Her head ached from thinking about the little children and no milk. She spoke out, "It's so unbelievable, poor little ones, what did they do before Kid's Café?"

She sipped her cold drink.

"My heart aches for them too."

∞

Meredith got the call from the Animal Shelter 10 days after she made her request.

"I'm Josie Chambers, welcome to our County Shelter."

They shook hands.

"A little surprised I got called so soon, expected it would be a while," Meredith smiled to her.

Meredith heard the incessant barking of the dogs throughout the facility.

She leaned into Josie and said, "I'm kinda having a hard time with the noise, just not used to it."

"Right," Josie turned to her, "we learn to tune out. Here we are, this golden retriever got injured on a ranch. Take a look, she might be a bit smaller dog than you requested. She's got a broken leg; the owner just left her with us, not getting the bone set. So of course we took her to the vet. No one's been willing to foot the bill for getting her shots, spaying and paying us back for the vet setting her leg. She's such a sweetheart; all the owner told us was that she ran super fast, actually helping out with cattle. From what the vet says he's afraid her speedy running days are over."

"Possible abused, or not cared for very well?"

"That's sounds about right, Meredith, but we got her cleaned up real good."

"Our family had a sweet husky/collie while I was growing up, such a loyal and happy companion for us. I'll check with my husband about this little lady and let you know by tomorrow afternoon. Can we take her out to see how her leg's healing, a limp?"

Josie confirmed by taking the dog walking on a leash around the facility that the leg was nearly ready to lose the cast. Meredith saw the dog only having a slight limp.

Colin said yes, and Meredith called the shelter. The spaying and all the shots got arranged with the vet. Earlier she picked up the needed food and supplies before coming to the shelter. The pet feed store carried the particular food, the only food that the dog would eat since it came to the shelter.   The shelter called her after the vet removed Jeeper's cast.

"The staff's been telling this little lady that she's going to a new home with her new name," Josie spoke out. "So she's heard her new name a few times, but might be that she won't respond to it right away, uh, until she gets used to you, your husband, and her new surroundings. She understands sit, stay, and lie down and is cooperative with those three voice signals."

Jeepers sat in the back seat of Meredith's SUV. The dog continued to shake the whole way from the shelter to the Sanderson farm. Meredith felt edgy, with a flippy tummy, "I'm afraid, Jeepers, that this is gonna be harder than I thought," she turned back, talking to the dog.

"I'm gonna let you get out slow-like. I don't want to hurt your healing leg."

Jeepers seemed to understand as Meredith gently helped the dog to the ground. Meredith had the leash around her own neck. She transferred the end of the leash to Jeeper's new collar and dog tags and held on to the other end. They walked around the front of the home and went inside via the front steps and front door.

Meredith took the leash off, "OK, Jeepers, you can go explore."

She listened as the dog pattered across the wood floors staying right beside her.

"Yes, that's the answer, get her nails cut often, so she doesn't clatter so much or scratch the floors. We won't have that noise, OK Jeepers?"

The dog cocked her head and looked into Meredith's eyes.

Meredith nodded, "I think you understand everything I'm telling you, Jeepers."

Meredith spent 15 minutes showing Jeepers around inside.

"Here's your water and food containers, here in the mud room. I'll bet you're thirsty."

She poured tap water from a pitcher into the water dish. Jeepers lapped every bit of it up. Meredith made coffee and drank a cup.

"Time to show you what we've done out back so you won't have to be tied up."

Meredith turned on the electric fence around a quadrant of the back yard, the area Colin decided was where Jeepers needed to stay. She led the dog from the mud room out back to the fenced in area.

"Jeepers, this is where you need to stay. You can't leave this part of the yard, OK?"

Before very many minutes the dog understood. Go past a particular area and she would get an electric shock. It was strong enough to discourage Jeepers from trying to leave an area again.

After Meredith ate dinner, she fed Jeepers. With Jeepers' leash on, they went for a walk around the home and up and down the lane coming into the property. By now the dog stopped shaking.

"Your new home, Jeepers, welcome; you represent a memory from my past, a sweet memory," Meredith knelt down and hugged her around the neck.

Jeepers gave her a sloppy slup across her face. Meredith laughed and hugged Jeepers again.

"How are you two getting along?"

"Hey Colin, good, I think she's even got her territory marked out for pee and poop."

"Good, I guess this will start to prepare us for a baby and a baby's ways."

"When you comin' home?"

"Tomorrow, I have three legislative visits, should be in by dinner. Grades all done?"

"Uh huh, said my goodbyes to my students, and I told them I'd miss them.

I mentioned that I hoped to return after a couple of years. Both classes finally asked me if I was having a baby. They felt a little shock when I told them when."

"You don't even look pregnant now, one student spoke out."

"Oh, but I am," I replied back to him.

"The emphatic way I said it made the whole class laugh. And hey, I did one thing with my AP kids; I shared a tiny bit about my last big project in the Air Force before I retired. Actually one of my students guessed what it was after I gave the class a clue."

"Hey, I don't even know what that project was."

"So I'll share with you, like I did with the students, fuel, developing special fuels now for our planes, and for new planes coming up, something the Air Force's been working on and working on, since we could take our minds a little bit away from the whole terrorism situation."

℘

"I'm home."

"Upstairs, Colin, with our new family member."

Colin took the steps up to the second floor two at a time. She stood in their bedroom. He went to Meredith for a hug and kiss. He felt a presence next to her and looked down. A golden dog stood close to Meredith. She shook and shook as she edged even closer to her new owner.

"She's super scared, Colin, did the same thing with me when I brought her home from the shelter."

They both got down on their knees.

"Jeepers, this is Colin. He lives here too. He's my husband. You'll get used to seeing him here sometimes, and then he's gone sometimes. He's a state representative for Iowa."

Colin watched Jeepers cock her head and look into his eyes.

"Hey, I think she understands everything you just told her about me."

Meredith patted Jeepers' head, "Pretty sure you're right about that."

They laughed together as Meredith hugged Jeepers.

"Super swell, Meredith, now you have two to hug, me and our dog."

As Meredith made dinner, Jeepers and Colin went all over the home. He found out where her food and water were located and where she liked to sleep at night, in a dog bed between the kitchen and mud room. Meredith watched from the French doors as Colin and Jeepers strolled around the perimeter of the backyard with the electric fence mechanism.

"Well, that's a success," he smiled to Meredith after they came back inside.

"I'm so glad you set that up. We don't have time to go chasing after a dog."

"Right, since she's a little disabled, she won't be running after big animals, real fast or far."

ഇ

Meredith stood with Colin in front of the small office space that fronted onto Porttown's main street.

"So this is where it all happens."

"Uh huh, it's pretty quiet now but by the time baby comes, the campaign will be in full swing. There'll be posters inside and out, and posters where people gather. Five of my favorite restaurants promised to have my posters."

"Signage?"

"A little, but not on any corporate property, that's a no-no. And I send one bright and colorful mailer to all addresses in our community and one other in my district."

Colin unlocked the door and ushered her in.

"How to get the word out?"

"The Porttown paper, a lot of people here still read a paper, the important stuff of the paper is online. I have a website, with my philosophy and what I stand for; there's lots of info now, since this will be my third run. I had a lot to do with some of the agendas that got passed. That's all part of the What I Stand For section of my website. It's also on the mailer I send out. Plus I have a ton of speaking engagements coming up in my district; I know so many people. It's more fun now, pretty tough sledding my first go round. But people know me now, that helps."

"Will I need to be with you sometimes?"

"Right, for the big stuff, I have a tentative calendar, that my campaign manager and I work on. Let's sit down and I'll explain."

"Tell me."

"Like with my first two elections, I pick a young person (campaign manager) who is in need of an internship."

"Where from?"

"Iowa State's Political Science program."

"Wow, how did that happen?"

Colin went on to explain his visit with the Political Science Department Head in 2007 and how that prof helped him get an outstanding intern each time Colin requested help.

"I've had two great interns, and I have every confidence this young man will fill the need for this reelection. I have a proven ability to raise a good amount of campaign money from a large pool of potential donors. Some of the folks at our reception, and at the New Year's Eve dance last year, those are donors, plus there are lots of others within the district."

"Wow, and you certainly have name recognition. I know that people vote for a name they know."

"Right," Colin nodded to her.

"I gotta learn to step up, Colin, I could help out where I'm needed."

"Well, we'll see, there's a baby for us."

"And the person in the other party?"

"Looks like a possible newcomer, that party is having trouble finding someone to run against me on the other side. I still gotta be careful and work my butt off to get reelected, remember nothin's certain."

She smiled to him as she came close to kiss his cheek, "Wow, that is for sure."

"And the money."

"You're keeping exact records?"

"Uh huh, actually running all the money through one of the CPA's at the firm we both use in Porttown. After $750, monies are disclosed to the Iowa Ethics and Campaign Disclosure Board."

"Good Colin, I always wondered how that got handled. I'm so glad you put that in someone else's hands, the CPA."

"Has to be that way, legal and transparent. And of course there's a software program, that I've used now for all campaigns, which really takes care of every aspect of the campaign, especially the money situation. My intern knows the program, it's what he used for a project at State. And by the way he and the other two young people I used, highly recommended by the profs in the Poly Sci department. The three of them know each other and trade concerns."

"Still?"

"Uh huh, it was a very big deal for each of them to be involved in my campaigns. The first two loved what they were doing."

She touched his arm, "Hey, that's just so awesome; they learned a lot from you."

"And me, from them."

She gazed about the room, got up and checked the back area, and bathroom.

"This place's gonna rock, hey, none of my business, but you do get compensation for your legislative work, right?"

"Yeah, we haven't discussed it, but Iowa pays me 25K and per diem, for my efforts January through May."

Meredith calculated in her head, "So," she paused, "covers your apartment in Des Moines, plus a little for food and events there."

"That's just about it; I live frugal-like at the capitol."

"I know you do; this is an enormous effort for all of us in the state of Iowa. I'm just beginning to fathom all that."

"You appreciate me."

"Yes, I do."

Colin stood and scooted their chairs back under the table. Meredith stepped to him and gave him her wide smile. She hugged him, a strong hug, and they kissed. Leaving the office they held hands as they walked to his SUV.

"Hey, Colin," two people mentioned as they stopped to greet Meredith and him.

Colin remembered their names and introduced them to Meredith. They exchanged information about their respective corn crops. They wished Colin good luck with the crop and his reelection.

"Take care, would appreciate your votes," he waved.

The two nodded their heads to him and smiled in acknowledgment.

"More people recognize me, than I recognize them, I got lucky remembering their names."

"You can't get to know everyone, Colin."

"But my public knows me, what I stand for."

∾

Colin and Meredith asked Adam and Amanda Cowden to dinner at the Sanderson farm, a possible date night for them. They came without their sons.

"This'll give you a chance to relax for a little bit," Colin nodded as they stood together in the kitchen.

"We're happy that we have this time with you," Amanda smiled to them.

Adam watched Colin barbecue on the back porch as they chatted. He turned and turned the chicken and vegetable kabobs until they cooked to his satisfaction. Amanda stirred the rice concoction as Meredith finished slicing the strawberries for the spinach/ strawberry salad. Jeepers sat in the corner of the kitchen. Her eyes kept track of what the two ladies accomplished.

"You know, she understands everything we're saying to each other," Meredith giggled as she turned to Jeepers.

Amanda watched as Jeepers cocked her head to one side and looked up into Meredith's eyes from the distance.

"You're right, she does understand. You got yourself one smart dog."

"We just gotta ask," Meredith smiled to Amanda and Adam after they finished their meal and sat on the back porch with their drinks.

"Tips for our little one, when he or she arrives, I've not been around kids much; I love my high schoolers, and the little ones at Kid's Café. I was in an adult kind of world, until I taught at the Academy."

"Hey, we learned the hard way, keep your baby up as much as possible during the day, you know, just the not-too-long morning and afternoon naps. That way babe'll learn that nighttime's for sleeping. The 10 p.m. and 2 a.m. feedings, then 6 a.m., well by our second child, we got baby to sleep from 10 to 5 within about 7 weeks."

"So you two still had some sane moments for your first son, after the second was born, right?"

"We had tough lessons with number one. Get on a schedule."

"Got it, Amanda, the old military background, it'll help me with that," Meredith moved to Amanda and hugged her shoulder.

"Enjoy your child, every second, because baby changes day by day, especially the first 15-18 months."

"It must be different now," Meredith paused, "especially for you."

"Yeah, little ones grow up so fast, in Pre-K at 4, kindergarten at 5."

"A quick game of Hearts?" Colin inquired as they all came in from the porch.

"Sounds great," Adam responded, "I gotta take a break before the cherry cheesecake. The meal was outstanding," he rubbed his tummy and murmured, "uuummm."

They played cards, then had dessert, and then a final game of cards. The four of them talked a little about the upcoming election, but the two couples kept the conversation light, inquiring about Meredith and her military life.

"Hearts, great fun, thank you Meredith and Colin," Amanda hugged Meredith and then Colin. The men shook hands, and Adam hugged Meredith.

"Lots comin' down the pike for you two," Adam nodded and smiled to them as they got ready to leave.

"I'm sure we really haven't got a clue," Colin started to laugh, with the three of them joining.

"Right about that," Amanda commented as they left. "Let us know; we can help out, the babe, the reelection."

"Thanks," Colin nodded to them.

℃

"So, the deal is, 4th of July committee's just decided that the symphony needs to be part of the program this year at City Park, late in the afternoon."

"Really?"

"Yup, do you think you could play, uh, a smaller symphony group 'cause some folks will be on vacation?"

"Sure, I'll be around, for sure, Phil, you kinda warned me that this happens every once in a while with the symphony."

"It does."

Meredith stood out in the backyard watching Jeepers' slight limp as she walked around near Meredith. She kept the phone to her ear.

"Practice?"

"One, we'll meet at the practice hall."

At the appointed date and time, the smaller group, about 50, met together. The high school choir joined them.

The conductor addressed the group, "We're gonna have you, choir, sing the *Star Spangled Banner* as we play to start off the ceremony. I know the whole crowd will join in. And at the end of this short concert, the choir'll sing *America* as we finish up."

The symphony practiced exactly as they would for the performance. More choir members showed up than the conductor expected.

"Wow," Phil nodded to them, "all your voices really add to the beginning and end of the performance, and when the audience joins in, it'll be great, thank you, choir."

The conductor bowed to the choir, and began clapping his hands with the symphony members adding their applause.

❧

Colin arrived in time to meet Meredith at City Park for the festivities on the Fourth. A large crowd of community folks enjoyed the food and camaraderie. After Colin ate with her, he got up and began to work the crowd. She watched, amazed at the numbers of people who greeted him with a smile and a handshake.

"This is certainly the kind of event that he needs to be a part of," she thought.

At the appointed time Meredith played with the symphony. The music took her, as it always had, to a special place in her mind, a place where she could see her Raymer family, smiling and waving little American flags, as they once did. As they finished, with hearing the last strains of *America*, Meredith teared up, a lump forming in her throat, as it did during parade formation when she was a military officer. She held tight to her French horn, "Thanks, God, for your gift to me, of being an American."

ℯ℣

The summer days flew along for Meredith. She loved working at the Kid's Café. She and Colin finished the childbirth classes. They went out to dessert after the final class with another couple who also were having their first child. Everyone shared their concerns.

"We're a lot older, so we kinda see all this in a bit of a different light. We also don't have the money issues you two have. But once you go back to work and baby goes to child care, I think you'll see everything'll get easier, without quite so many pressures," Colin commented.

"Yeah," the husband blew out a breath, "that is my sincere hope. So far my wife's pregnancy's been smooth, without incident."

"We've been lucky, the same way, but because of my family's history, we had an amniocentesis done, to help ensure all was OK as far as we all know."

On the drive home, Meredith turned to Colin, "So, we've talked to one couple who have kids, and one couple who's about to. I'm excited for our little one to arrive."

"Me too," Colin took his right hand from the steering wheel and touched Meredith's cheek.

Meredith turned back to Ty and Jeepers. Jeepers sat up on the back seat floor looking up into Ty's bright blue eyes as he sat in his baby seat, facing into the back seat.

"Hey, Jeepers, are you and Ty OK back there?"

It remained quiet in the back seat. The baby and dog became Meredith's constant companions as they did chores away from the farm. Meredith made a deliberate attempt to have places to go with two-week-old Ty every morning, keeping the afternoons for Ty's quiet naptime in his own bedroom. As Amanda mentioned to her, Meredith did get her boy on an eating schedule. Something went missing in Meredith's breast milk. It did not satisfy Ty. Now Meredith bottle fed him a soy formula milk. He drank it with gusto, and it held him for the four hours until the next feeding.

And Colin or Meredith read books to Ty every night, from the night he got home from the hospital. Meredith kept music on all day long and into the evening, everything from jazz to classical to rock to blue grass and country. Jeepers became unbelievably devoted to the baby, staying close by wherever he or Meredith happened to be. Meredith and Colin also included Ty in all their conversations, having him sit close in his baby seat as they ate their meals. They knew it would not be long before Ty would sit in his high chair and have meals with them.

Many evenings they would walk with Ty and show him the corn field. Jeepers stayed close by as Meredith would point out the growing corn.

"It's gonna be ready pretty darn soon, young man," Colin would say to Ty. Ty looked into his dad's pools of blue, eyes that matched Ty's own eyes.

"This is your future, little man, the next generation of corn farmer, if that's what you want to do. We'll not push you; you'll make up your own mind."

"After college," Meredith added.

"Right."

In the fading sun they could both see a little blonde fuzz begin to appear on the top of Ty's head.

"You'll stay blonde for a while, right my boy?"

He handed Ty to Meredith.

She looked to Colin, "It'll probably darken a bit as he gets older, both Conner and I were towheads when we were little."

Colin put his arm around Meredith as they returned to their back porch.

"My dear God, how I love you, Meredith. It's been such a joy to be with you, this summer. You've handled everything, well, with such organization, you plan so well. And I know I'm on my way in my reelection. We just work so good as a unit, you, me, Tyler. I'm so happy you have him out and about every day, to the library, grocery store, spending time with Amanda, working with the cow and calf. I know her son is lots older but he and Ty seem to get along. Ben talks to Ty, plays with his toys nearby, Ty seems like Jeepers, just understands everything we and everyone else tell him."

Meredith turned to him, "I love you, Colin, and yes I've loved having you with me. I know that's changing, but you've had a chance to get to know your little son. He'll change a lot while you're in Des Moines. I know you'll get home as much as you can."

സ

"OK, Jeepers and Ty, ready to head out, see what's happening with our favorite cow and calf?"

Meredith cradled Ty against her front, in a carrier Ty seemed to like. She faced him out so he could see everything.

"You two are the most observant kid and dog I've ever seen," she smiled to Ty and looked down and smiled again to Jeepers.

Meredith and Ty moved along at a quick pace; Jeepers did her best to keep up with them. Sometimes her leash strained tight until she caught up to them. Meredith opened the gate and closed it once they were inside the cow area.

Both the cow and calf lay on their sides, very near each other. Meredith moved close to them. They lay very still. Meredith squatted down, pressing her left hand against Ty so he would not flop forward. With her right hand she touched the cow's neck. She could not feel any movement, no breath, nothing.

She raised up and went to the calf, same thing.

"Dear God, help me, what's happened to our animals?"

Tears squashed the outside of her eyes.

"I don't want to upset you two, Ty and Jeepers, so I'll stay calm. We need to leave right now."

She called the veterinarian's office that late October morning. She explained in a teary voice what she saw when she went to feed her animals. The receptionist assured her that Dr. Altermer would come out to the Sanderson farm to diagnose the situation, hopefully later that day.

He did arrive as Tyler got up from his afternoon nap. This time Meredith kept Jeepers in the farm house. Whatever it was, she didn't want the dog to have a problem.

Meredith held Ty as she watched the vet and his assistant examine the cow and calf. She showed the several bales of feed that the previous owner suggested that she feed the cattle after she took ownership.

"The feed?" the vet asked.

"Uh huh, corn stalks, small grains, sorghum, I've fed that to them for the week they've been in my care."

"Meredith, I'll need to do an autopsy, to see what happened here. We'll also test samples of the feed you've given them."

"Gosh, Dr. Altermer, any clues as to what's happened?"

He saw the worry in her wideset eyes and the crease of concern between her eyes.

"Not clear until I do my testing and send the information off. It'll be several days; I been carrying a big load, for a sick veterinarian, who's finally back on his feet."

"That's rough, and it's corn harvest also."

The vet smiled to Meredith and nodded, "Always the way things go."

"When will the cow and calf," Meredith swallowed hard, "leave?"

"Tomorrow morning, we won't bother you. I've got someone lined up to remove them from your property."

"Let's go back home, Ty, Jeepers will wonder what happened to us. Your dad, he'll be one tired toad, by the time he gets home."

Meredith and Colin ate very late that evening after they put Ty to bed. Meredith broke down as they started in on their beef stroganoff dinner.

"I'm so sad, Colin. We got excited about starting the cow-calf operation again. I feel like whatever happened's gotta be my fault."

"Dear one, don't do that. We have to wait for the lab's analysis, you know after the autopsy. I'm wondering about the feed, that's to be analyzed also."

As they cleaned up after the meal they finished their conversation.

"Bummed, this has been a super expensive experiment, Colin, that looks like a failure. I don't think I want to try this again, at least not for a while. I gotta look after Ty, and you, you're so busy with your reelection campaign. I think

I took on too much." She nodded her head. "Hey how's harvest going, do you think?"

"Great, weather's holding, Ted mentioned you and Ty stopped by at the Raymer place, to see the cutting on a close field."

"We did, I still can't tell really what's going on, just trust our workers."

"As I do, I just kinda watch, been awhile since I've been on the equipment."

"I'm so sorry, Colin, you just don't need this in your life right now."

He took her in his arms as they stood together, looking out the French doors at the trees beginning to show their fall colors.

"I love you, these precious times when I have you and Ty close."

She stood on her tiptoes and kissed him. They hurried up to their bedroom.

"He'll be hungry soon. Right now, I hunger for you. So happy to be able to make love to you after that time away as you healed."

"I'm happy too," she smiled as she looked up into his eyes. He eased into her as they became one.

℘

"There sure is wonder in this baby's eyes," Julie turned to Meredith as she spoke.

"Fer sure, he's a super observant little guy; we talk directly to him, like he's another adult."

"He'll talk early, betcha," Ty's grandma kissed him on the top of his head. She continued to hold him as they stood by the kitchen counter. "I always talked to you and Conner; you're so smart, just picked up what adults said, and it rubbed off on Conner. Once you learned something, Conner learned it. You were one great teacher, Meredith."

She smiled to her mom, "And I thought it just was being a little sister to Conner, and helping out."

"Helping out, oh Meredith, you always did that."

"It's like that now, Mom, Colin, me, Ty, Jeepers, we're just a good team together."

"I'm impressed at how Jeepers watches over Ty. She's just a really devoted and trustworthy little dog."

"Just like Jeepers was," they said in unison, and then laughed to each other.

"You haven't told me what happened with your cow and calf, Meredith."

"Oh, Mom, so sad to lose them both. It was the bales of grain I was feeding them, same stuff as what the previous owner did. But that diet, it was accumulated nitrate levels, too high. Both animals died of nitrate poisoning. I'm not gonna try that experiment again."

Like last time, Julie came for a two day visit with her new grandbaby and his folks.

"Say goodbye to Colin for me; I know he's crazy busy."

"I will, Mom."

She and Ty stood by Julie's rental car.

Julie hugged them.

"So proud of you, Meredith, as you have all your life, you're doing great with Ty, keeping Colin headed in the right direction with his campaign."

"Thanks, Mom, I look at it all now like all the tasks I juggled back in my Air Force days." She stepped away from her mom, "'Cept now, this is my precious family I'm dealing with. God's been with me, every step of the way."

"I'll try to come next spring. This little guy will change so much. Keep shooting me e-mail pics."

"I will, Mom, we love you."

Meredith took one of Ty's hands and waved it to his grandma. She smiled, waved back, and headed for the airport.

☙

"Thank you, Jess."

Meredith gave her friend a hug.

"I know you've wanted to spend time with Ty again, I'm afraid he's already down for the count. I'll be home after the announcement's made.   Colin'll still be at the campaign office."

"You know he'll win again, Meredith, don't you?"

"I don't know that; I'm still so new to the whole political scene, which he handles with ease.   For sure, nothing is certain until all the votes have been counted."

"That's exactly correct."

Midnight came, and the final count arrived. The crowd in Colin's reelection office went silent. Garrett, Colin's campaign manager, stood next to Colin. Meredith held Colin's hand.

"Unbelievable how excited I feel," she thought as she gazed around the room and then cast her eyes to her husband's face. She watched his smile.

"He must suspect," she whispered.

Colin and Meredith hugged after they heard the announcement.

"Thank you for everything, Meredith," he whispered.

Meredith felt her lips connect with his in a soft and comforting kiss. He took her right arm and raised it up with his left arm. They waved to the crowd.

"Two more years, two more years," Meredith heard the chant begin in the crowd. Everyone repeated it a few more times and then applause broke out around the room.

Colin spoke after they quieted. He talked about what his state legislature and he needed to address for the sessions in '13 and '14.

"You'll get 'er done, Colin," one person in the crowd shouted out as he finished talking.

They went around the room shaking hands with everyone who stayed on at that late hour. Meredith watched Colin as he continued to smile, shake hands, and pat folks on the back.

"He's in his element; this is sure where he needs to be," Meredith mentioned to the older lady who stood next to her as Colin continued to work the room after Meredith stepped away.

The lady touched Meredith's arm, "Just love him."

She spoke in a quiet tone close so that Meredith could hear her.

"I will do that," she smiled to the lady.

Meredith got her coat and left. Colin knew she planned to go so she could be home for Ty's 5:30 feeding.

"My boy, he's sleeping through the night," she told Jess after she arrived home. "Thanks for watching over our son," Meredith hugged her.

"It's going to be my pleasure to watch this tyke grow up."

Meredith helped Jess with her coat.

"Colin, happy?"

"Very," Meredith replied.

After she watched Jess drive down the lane, Meredith made a small pot of decaf coffee. She drank a cup and ate a chocolate chip bar.

"Tyler Jack, sleep well, I'll be ready to feed you in a little while," she whispered as she gazed at him in his crib.

Colin arrived home within a half hour. They spooned together, their excitement quickly changing as sleep caught them.

℃

Right before Christmas Colin and the governor sat down in Colin's office at the state house. The governor requested the meeting. They talked about the upcoming legislative agenda. He asked Colin how he liked serving as a judge in four different school science fairs around the Des Moines area.

"This'll be my fifth year of helping out, and always," he paused and smiled to the governor, "am astounded at how bright our kids are, and the ideas they come up with at these fairs, incredible!"

Colin went on to explain a science experiment from a 5th grade girl that he remembered in detail.

"My wife, Meredith, retired Air Force lieutenant colonel, chemistry was her field. She loved it from the time she was a little kid doing experiments out in her dad's barn. Back in the day STEM wasn't a part of hardly anyone's push in the middle and high school curriculums.

But today, there's a big emphasis, in helping, especially girls and underrepresented youngsters, enjoy science, technology, engineering, and math, uh, the STEM program. Meredith took over last spring semester, for a teacher who moved away from our high school in Porttown. She taught one chemistry class and one Advanced Placement chemistry class. She and the students really enjoyed each other and the class. Oh, and she taught chemistry at the Air Force Academy."

"You've been active in our state and national Corngrower's Associations, right?"

"Correct, I've pretty much been all over as Iowa's president (before that the treasurer) of the group. At the national level, I'm serving as a member of a corngrower's commission working with trade groups from the countries of Germany, South Korea, and Vietnam. It's all about corn, and, of course, ethanol."

Colin freshened his and the governor's coffee. They exchanged information about their families.

"You've got lots to look forward to with your young son. Love him and his mother, love them well."

"Thanks, I hope I've helped you in some way, getting to know me better."

"I have and I appreciate your time, in coming to Des Moines, at this busy Christmas time."

"This'll be Meredith and my first Christmas with our son, Tyler."

"Thanks for the coffee and Happy Holidays to you and yours."

They shook hands. Colin noticed how much the governor's eyes brightened as their conversation went along.

"Sheesh, not sure I understand what that was all about," he shook his head as he walked back to his place in Des Moines.

℘

"Dear one, I'll stay in Des Moines for the night, a couple things I need to catch up on. My meeting with the governor, I'll share when I get home. I talked some about you."

"OK, I'll look forward to hearing about all that. Be safe driving home tomorrow."

"I will, hugs and kisses to Ty."

"I love you."

"And I love you."

℥

Colin fed Ty as Meredith put the pumpkin pie in the oven.

"Saving it for Christmas dinner?"

"Right, we got cookies and fudge to eat for dessert right now."

After she set the timer, she went to Colin and kissed him on the top of his head. She patted Ty's feet as he continued to suck down the soy milk.

"Pretty soon, real food, right Ty?"

"Uh huh, warm rice cereal for starters, I'm pretty sure you'll like that."

Ty directed his eyes away from his dad up to his mom.

Meredith giggled, "Yeah, his eyes tell me he's soon ready for real food."

Jeepers and Meredith sat on the rug away from the warm fire. Colin sat close to them, holding Ty and reading *Twas the Night before Christmas* to his audience. Meredith gazed from the sparkling lighted tree to her family.

"Thank you God, for your blessings on us all," she whispered.

Meredith clapped as Colin finished. Jeepers sat closer to her. She patted the dog and touched Colin's shoulder and Ty's leg.

"Your special Christmas present, Ty, which we'll talk to you about one day."

Meredith held the small ornament for Ty and Colin to see. A tiny teddy bear held a flag with the wording, BABY'S FIRST CHRISTMAS. On the back of the flag Meredith etched in 2012 with a fine point marker.

"I want to give you a new ornament every year, Ty, to match what you are interested in. It'll be fun for your dad and me to go through your history through ornaments."

"Great idea, Meredith," Colin caught her eyes and nodded to her. "And, little guy, you'll change so much year to year." He looked into his son's bright blue eyes, "So mommy's gonna hang the ornament on the tree now, OK?"

Ty watched his mom hang the ornament in a spot he could see also when he sat in his baby seat. Jeepers moved close to Ty and lay down.

They both watched as Meredith returned to her place and sat down next to Colin.

"Meredith, does Ty play with any toys yet?"

"Not yet, but he sometimes grabs a set of plastic rings that he will soon be chewing on."

"Does he have a teddy bear?"

"Yip, a small one, I don't want anything in his crib, but teddy sits on Ty's toy shelf in his room."

"Uh huh, I gotta check that. I think it's about time that I get him big Legos.   I remember how much I loved my blocks and Lincoln Logs and the projects I would construct. At the Cowden's they have tons of Legos."

"Good idea for his constructing projects, I wasn't a builder, just wanted to see what combined with what, mixing up my dirt mud pies with various grasses. Mom started to give me baking soda, sugar, salt, stuff from the kitchen to experiment with, well I was in heaven."

ℴℴ

"A lovely meal, Meredith, thanks. And you remembered my request for a special wine with a story behind it, good story!" Sam exclaimed. The four of them laughed together. Tyler fell asleep in Jess's arms as they moved away from the table to clear it.

Colin took Tyler from Jess and put him down for his afternoon nap. He returned as they got their desserts and sat near the warm fire.

"When do you head out, Colin?"

"Two important items before I go, my dear one's 40th birthday coming up, and New Year's Eve and Day, uh, football and relaxation. Then I'll head for Des Moines."

"Colin knows," she touched his shoulder, "I want a quiet birthday, just like I've had this quiet Christmas, time with my family, before he goes."

"Quite a change since last Christmas," Jess smiled to them, "the three of you at my home. There's been a wedding and a reception and two new members come into the Sanderson family, Jeepers and Tyler Jack."

Jeepers perked her head up as she heard her name.

"She's incredibly loyal to Meredith and to Tyler, always close by them when she's not outside or sleeping."

"Yay, Jeepers," Meredith clapped to the dog. "You've been one of my wishes come true."

"Hey, what about me?" Colin whimpered to her.

"Yes, you too, precious one," Meredith leaned and kissed his cheek, "my wish that you have a third term, yes that wish's coming true."

"We'll toast to that at the New Year's Eve Ball; you two are joining us?" Sam asked.

"We are," Colin nodded to them. "We've found a sweet teen, 15, who will watch over Ty and spend the night in our guest bedroom. She really likes the little guy. They get along great, and we've had Alexa sit for us several times before."

"Great, it'll be fun for the four of us, out in the public eye, which Colin you'll be doing more and more of, I feel certain."

"OK, oh great predictor," Colin bowed his head to Jess.

℘

"Meredith, we gotta talk."

"Got it, when'll you be home from your meeting?"

"About one; I'll have eaten."

Colin did arrive home at one, and they had their talk. Meredith felt her mind spinning out of control; she made a deliberate attempt to pray instead. It worked for a little while.

"We need to be at the governor's office by 10:30 tomorrow."

They arrived five minutes early. Meredith kept praying. Colin finally explained to her that the governor and he met briefly some days before that. He mentioned a couple of topics they discussed.

Meredith held Ty as Colin introduced them to the governor and two other officials. The governor made his requests, and Colin responded to the requests.

"Our lives are changing, maybe for a long time to come," Meredith mused as they headed back to Porttown.

She looked over to Colin. He turned to her and smiled.

"You've always said you'd help me along the way. This sure isn't the way I planned my political career. But you've agreed to what I said I would do."

"Loyalty, faith in you, in your abilities, hope for our futures, Colin, and love for each other and for that little tyke in the backseat."

She turned back to see Ty sleeping in his baby seat.

Sam and Jess met them in a corner of a little family restaurant the next day for lunch. The noisy lunch crowd enjoyed their food.

After they ordered, Jess said, "Spill, Meredith, what do you and Colin need to talk to us about?"

"So, Colin's accepted a challenge."

Colin watched Sam fold his arms across his chest, "State Representative Sanderson, third term reelect, what in the world could that challenge be?"

"I'll talk quiet-like, you folks too."

He gave them the eye.

"Lieutenant governor's resigned, effective two days ago. The three of us drove to Des Moines yesterday to meet with the governor and two other officials. He asked me to be his nominee to take over the role of Lieutenant Governor for our state."

Sam and Jess looked at each other. Their eyes widened as they both gazed at Colin.

"Oh my goodness," Jess stopped talking, just continuing to look at him.

"And, a decision?" Sam asked.

"Yeah, Meredith and I didn't even need to discuss it. I saw her shining eyes and the nod of her head after he asked me. That settled it in my mind. I told him I would be honored to be his nominee."

"And what would that entail?"

"A lot," Meredith added.

"He gave us the six pages of duties involved in the role. He said that in some states the lt. governor has a small role. But not the case here, he and the state of Iowa are asking a lot of a lt. governor. He told us that he wants a strong leader for the job."

"What happens next?" Jess asked.

"Confirmation hearing (I imagine bipartisan), then nominated and approved by both the State House and State Senate."

"After we got home last night we sat down and went through the duties together."

"So, Meredith are you ready to hold down the farm and your farm acreage so Colin can fulfill the duties?"

"Please guys, he's got a ways to go before anything's decided, remember that. Gosh, I am, I did so gosh almighty much in my military positions. If it happens, the three of us, our time together, will just have to be very precious. God's in charge."

Colin added, "We both believe that, He's in charge, today, and through all of our tomorrows."

Meredith nodded as she continued in her quiet voice, "And please, this is just for you two. Whatever happens, news will probably not be released until after the confirmation process is completed."

℘

Colin stayed home with Ty so Meredith could attend the Christmas Eve service. She prayed a lot as the service proceeded. As always her favorite part was the end with the candles and the singing.

"I sure hope someday I can get back with the choir and play my French horn," she whispered as she walked with the congregation out into the snowy landscape.

Colin heard Christmas music in their home all through Christmas morning. He mixed up the stove top dressing to go with the turkey breast and gravy. Before they sat down to the early afternoon meal they talked to Julie, and then called Jess.

"Oh, my favorite couple, enjoy the peace and quiet of this beautiful day; I imagine the years coming will be filled with more people and a growing boy."

They had her on speaker phone.

"Big Legos for Ty?" Jess asked.

"Absolutely, I sat down on the floor with Meredith. We built a couple of items. Ty and Jeepers watched. I know he'll be diligently building towers and fun cars before we know it."

"Colin," Jess paused, "I, I think I need to stick my neck out, it's on my mind and in my heart, my adopted son, you will be our lieutenant governor."

"I'm not sure that's s'posed to comfort me, or scare the crap out'a me."

Meredith and Colin laughed to each other. They heard Jess join in over the phone.

"In my thoughts and prayers, you two are," she finished.

"We know that, and thanks, adopted mom." Colin assured her.

&

"Quick trip to Des Moines, be back in the morning for your birthday. What'cha want to do?"

Colin came up to Meredith and hugged her.

"I ordered wreaths for dad, Uncle Milt, and Conner's graves. Want me to get something for your family?"

She looked into his eyes, questioning him.

"Nah, it's OK, never done anything like that, and it's been just, such a long time ago. But I want to be with you and Ty when we go to the Raymer family's graves. It'll become a holiday tradition for the three of us."

She watched him shake his head.

"You'll not have to go out to the graves alone, for a long time Meredith."

"Great, I'll pick the wreaths up tomorrow. We'll be ready for you when you get home."

Colin arrived back at the farm midmorning the next day.

"You didn't ask why I went to Des Moines, want to know?"

"Course, glad you had a safe trip and back, Ty and I missed you last night."

"I found a little bit bigger apartment, this time just one bedroom, but roomier. I'm losing my old roommate. He's moved on to other endeavors."

"Close by?"

"Yeah, actually in the same apartment complex so it'll be easy to move my stuff, it's furnished, same as what I have now. I'm a married man with a child so I need something for the three of us, 'cause I'm hoping you'll be coming more often, at least for a little while."

"Jess seems pretty confident in what's going to happen with you."

"She sure does. I'm ready for whatever kind of questioning the house and senate throw at me."

Colin held Ty as Meredith carried the wreaths to the Raymer plots at Landview.

She put a wreath in front of the headstone on each of her family member's graves. She touched each headstone and said a prayer for the family member. Colin handed Ty to Meredith.

She moved her head closer to her son, "A beautiful, cold, but sunny day, so here Ty is where your grandpa, great uncle, and uncle rest. It's a beautiful spot. One day you'll stand here as we do now, and go round and round, seeing the land in all directions."

She turned and turned with Ty, viewing the snow-covered grass and the little hills popping up in the distance.

"Time to go," she nodded to Colin and Ty.

They trod along in the snow. Then Meredith remembered. Last year, after she left the wreaths at the graves she felt a presence. In her memory she turned and saw her dad, uncle, and brother walking next to her as she returned to the car. She moved her head to the right. Colin held Ty as they headed for the parked SUV. She felt burning tears trickle down her face.

"I miss my family, God, help me," Meredith thought. She stood still, unable to take a step or take a breath for a moment.

Colin held Ty a little tighter as he watched his wife with her tearful face. He stepped near her and put his free arm around her. She came in close and put her arms around Ty and Colin.

"You miss them, Meredith."

"Oh yes, really I do, it catches me up," she paused, then he heard her voice crack, "like now."

Meredith let go of her husband and son and stepped back. Colin reached out and brushed her tears away. She tried to smile to him, but her tears started afresh.

"I'll be OK in a minute; you two go on ahead. I'll be along."

Colin nodded to her. They walked to the car.

"There's my future, God, thank you for giving me the gifts of this man and this baby," she spoke out to the breeze moving her hair across her face.

⅋

"I've eaten in some of the most exotic places in the world, Colin. But I'm just a country girl, the hamburgers and fries at this little café are the best, just about my most favorite food in this wide world."

Colin and Meredith sat next to each other at the little restaurant.

"Hey, I remember you telling me some time since you returned to Porttown how much you liked this place."

"It's absolutely the perfect food for my birthday. We already had birthday cake and ice cream at home earlier today. Remember, dessert first."

"Yeah, that's right, dear one."

Meredith drove Alexa home after their dinner out. They talked about the junior play Alexa would star in.

"We'll come and see it, Alexa, I'm excited for you, reaching out to do all kinds of endeavors, just keep trying stuff."

"I will Meredith, thanks for the ride; I really like watching over Ty. He's a super cool little guy."

"Yeah, wait'll he can walk and talk."

They laughed together, "Uh huh, that'll be wild and crazy."

છ

"Wow, we should watch Hanks and Ryan in movies more often, you were so much fun tonight."

"Hey, birthdays just do that to me."

They turned to each other after their lovemaking, "This is a precious time; we'll be gone a lot from each other pretty soon."

"You'll be wanting to come to Des Moines more often. Meredith, I just can't comprehend what all is going to happen."

"A lot more will go on, besides the legislative session from January into May."

They spooned together as sleep took them.

છ

He held her close as a slow dance began. The smell of her hair and her perfume enticed his nose and caused his groin to ache in wanting her. He held her closer.

"Unbelievable, together now for over a year, I love you Meredith, each day I discover more and more about you."

"As I discover you, Colin, I pray for you, I get to be mom, and wife, and you may be representing the people of Iowa.   That's awesome, an awesome responsibility, a challenge for you."

The song ended and he still held her close.

"I am ready."

Meredith stepped back as he let her leave his arms. She smiled to him, looking up into his blue eyes and nodding.

The new year came and they toasted it with champagne and best wishes from the crowd at the country club. That first day of the year they hosted a gathering of the fifteen folks who helped Colin with his campaign for reelection. They brought their spouses, partners, and children for conversation and a buffet luncheon. Some folks watched the football games; others chatted while they enjoyed the delicious chow, including large mounds of chicken wings and curly fries. Again, Meredith and Colin used the caterers who helped with their wedding reception. They chose not to talk about the hearings Colin would be going through regarding the lieutenant governor position. Instead they wanted to thank all of Colin's helpers.

"They deserve our appreciation, for believing in you, Colin," Meredith mentioned after they helped the caterers clean up from the luncheon.

"Agreed, not sure how they'll react to the other news, if it happens."

ℂ

Colin called from Des Moines. He left them January 2nd. Today was the 10th.

"I'm in, Meredith, our lives, at least for the next few years are going to be different. They want you and Ty to be with me. We'll be introduced in front of the entire membership, senate and house.   It went, uh the confirmation hearing, faster than I expected, guess they want me."

"Hey, congratulations, Colin, of course they want you. Do you remember, back when you came to see me at school, after Tyler died, do you remember what you told me?"

"Pretty much," he paused, "I told you to work hard, keep trying, your hopes and dreams would continue to unfold."

"And I pass your words you gave me as we stood in the parking lot of that restaurant, I pass those words back to you; it's what you've done all your life, and look what's happened."

"Oh my gosh, Meredith, it's true for both of us."

℁

February arrived. Meredith and Ty spent one Saturday night with Colin at his apartment in Des Moines. And then Colin came home the next snowy Saturday morning. He wanted to celebrate their first anniversary with Meredith in their home. They grilled steaks.

"I want us to have the same meal we had the first time we were together in Porttown."

"Yeah, I hadn't been retired for very long. I felt very strange back in the civilian world."

Ty sat between them at the dining room table. They propped him up so he could sit in his highchair.

"The filets are, mmm, perfect. You're sure the grill master, Colin."

"The twice-baked potatoes, also yummy. Ty likes them too, the creamy potatoes mixed up with a little milk. Hey, you like some vegetables, don't you?"

Colin smiled to Ty.

"Did you see that, Meredith, he nodded to me, yeah, this kid knows exactly what we're sayin'."

"He's already making his mmm and ddd sounds, some of the first ones a little one says."

"For mommy and daddy?"

"That's right," she paused, "Daddy."

They laughed together and Ty joined in.

After they took turns reading to Ty in front of the fire, they put him to bed. They held hands, returning down the steps to the couch and the warmth of the fire. They held hands after Colin handed Meredith a single red rose. She put it on the armrest of the couch. They turned to each other.

"You, oh you Colin, can look in my eyes, reading my feelings and my thoughts."

"The words you say to me, Meredith, your loving words, they fill me up to the brim with joy."

"You are the love of my life, and you are also my very best friend."

"Dear one, wherever life is gonna take us, your embrace will always be my home. The light of your smile will be my comfort."

They held on tight to each other.

ROSES FOR MEREDITH

16-year-old college student, Meredith, receives a surprise, two rosebuds, one from Cole and the other from Tyler. Her delight in her chemistry major changes with one phone call. Meredith's dad asks her to move back home.

Meredith returns to Porttown after her spring semester to help with the fall corn crop. Her mother walks away. Meredith must cope with loss while taking care of her family. She works at a floral shop to replace her mother. Tyler spends time with Meredith that summer. They support and love each other; Tyler in his quest to be an engineer and pilot, and Meredith in her wish to study chemistry and become an Air Force officer.

An accident sidelines Meredith's dad. Colin steps up to help Meredith and her family. They, in turn, assist their neighbor, Colin, with his first corn harvest. Colin and Meredith know and care for each other from earlier times. They go out on several dates. Tyler flies himself to spend Thanksgiving with Meredith and her family. They express their happiness in being able to spend their next semesters together.

Meredith returns to State. Joy becomes despair. After a time Colin visits, bringing hope for her future.

About Cathleen

www.CathleenEllis.com

Cathleen Ellis is a Colorado native. She and her husband, John, live in the northern part of the state. They have four sons, three daughters-in-law, and four grandchildren. Cathleen draws the inspiration for her love stories from the lives of young people with whom she has lived and worked her entire life.